MW01715212

SMALL DETAILS

SMALL DETAILS

•

MARJORIE EVERITT

AVALON BOOKS
THOMAS BOUREGY AND COMPANY, INC.
401 LAFAYETTE STREET
NEW YORK, NEW YORK 10003

© Copyright 1993 by Marjorie Everitt
Library of Congress Catalog Card Number: 93-90434
ISBN 0-8034-9006-2
All rights reserved.
All the characters in this book are fictitious,
and any resemblance to actual persons,
living or dead, is purely coincidental.

PRINTED IN THE UNITED STATES OF AMERICA
ON ACID-FREE PAPER
BY HADDON CRAFTSMEN, SCRANTON, PENNSYLVANIA

SMALL DETAILS

Chapter One

Jenny removed the partially completed roof of Gillyflower Cottage. She peered at it closely, as if looking for birds' nests in the thatch, blew at it a few times to remove infinitesimal specks of dust and loose thatch, and put it carefully on the table.

Then, after staring at it thoughtfully for perhaps fifteen seconds, she pushed her oversize glasses back up on her nose and sighed. Something didn't seem right. She replaced the roof, fitting it gently over the pegs she had inserted—in a rather innovative way, she thought—in the side walls. Was it straight? It wasn't straight.

"Jennifer Blakemore, I wish you'd make up your mind. You're making it look as if a major earthquake has hit the Devonshire coast. You've had the roof and chimney apart five times in the last five minutes and the show starts in another five."

"Maybe five's my lucky number," Jenny mumbled. "Is it straight, Gilda? It's supposed to be straight."

"It has a beautiful, natural, cleverly contrived bow in the roofline to make it seem aged. You managed that very nicely. Other than that, it's straight. Quit worrying, hon.''

Gilda Scott rearranged four Victorian ladies in beribboned bustles and a small boy with a hoop within her glass case and grinned. ''Next time we do the same show, I'm going to ask to be assigned a space clear across the room from you. You're an incurable perfectionist!''

''Five minutes?'' Jenny squeaked in dismay as her mind registered that part of Gilda's comments. ''Did you say five minutes?'' She sneaked a quick, panicked look toward the door, where velvet ropes held back the crowd: mostly women with bright, eager eyes scanning the displays, and a tall man with a disinterested expression towering over the front phalanx. . . .

''Four,'' Gilda corrected, placing a two-inch toddler on a minute potty chair.

''I'll never be ready.''

''You'll be ready. You always are.''

She was, although her hands suddenly felt like Gulliver's gropings in the land of Lilliput. She plugged in the twelve-volt transformer that made Gillyflower Cottage come aglow with soft lights and quickly rearranged the impressive assortment of fine furnishings and accessories that graced her display table. She was smiling with surface confidence and good cheer when the throngs poured in, but she couldn't help sneaking peeks at the roofline of the cottage. *Was* it straight?

She had very little time to worry about it. The Friday-evening preview of the eighth annual New England Minifest Miniature Show and Sale (usually referred to as NEMMS in the interest of brevity) appeared to be a sellout. The promoters couldn't have fit another person into the large display rooms without a shoehorn.

The first couple of hours were unbelievably busy. She sold a good percentage of her stock, handed out brochures, and answered questions about her houses in general and Gillyflower Cottage in particular. Faces blurred. Her voice grew hoarse, her feet hurt, her glasses kept slipping down her nose.

And still they came, in droves and hordes. The words "cute" or "adorable" or "precious" could be heard frequently, but that was all right. Serious miniaturists used those words sparingly, aware of the amount of time and talent (and sometimes tears and trauma) that went into the best work.

The knot of people around her table seemed to thin slightly toward nine. Jenny looked up, able to see individual features for the first time. A little gray-haired woman stood a few feet away from her table, staring at Gillyflower Cottage, face rapt. A man stood behind her, half turned, looking out over the other displays with an air of resignation. She thought it was the same man she had seen in the crowd of waiting people at opening time. It was the same slightly bored look, anyway.

"If you have any questions, just ask," Jenny said softly. The woman started and seemed to come back from far away.

"Just admiring," she murmured. "What a beautiful house."

"It will be, I hope, when I've finished. It's copied from an actual house in Devon, England."

"You do that? Copy real houses, I mean?" Jenny realized that the small woman wasn't really gray-haired. More of a silver, rather glowing sixtyish silver. Her hair, eyes, even her suit and scarf seemed to blend together. The effect rendered her almost invisible—until you noticed the glow.

"Oh, yes. My father and I do them together."

The gray-silver woman stepped up closer to the table and picked up one of Jenny's business cards. "Could you possibly do a saltbox?" she asked. "A copy of a real one, that is?"

Jenny laughed. "Saltboxes are easy. Easier than thatched cottages, anyway." The man—young, dark, probably the woman's son—had turned back and was listening to them now, an uneasy frown drawing his brows together. Jenny glanced briefly at him and then back at the woman. She had seen that look before and knew it was best to ignore it. "Yes, I do commissions."

"They are quite expensive, I would imagine." The words were thoughtful. "But still, how long does it take to build one?" Her voice was silvery, just like her appearance, each little word perfectly formed and enunciated. Jenny smiled at her, thinking perhaps illogically that she would be a fine miniaturist.

"It depends. I usually need about six months to a year to do a complete house—with windows, doors, flooring, and all that. A shell would be a little less."

"And the cost?" the woman asked. She had a gleam

in her eye now, and hardly hid it with a blink when Jenny quoted her a range of prices.

This was more than could be said for the man behind her.

"Mother!" he exclaimed, and Jenny could have sworn there was real horror in his voice. "You're not! You wouldn't! What would you do with it?"

"I would love it, of course," his mother said with a note of firm precision designed to squelch his horror. "Don't be such a stuffed shirt, Bennet."

Actually, Jenny thought as she really looked at him for the first time, Bennet didn't look much like her idea of a stuffed shirt. He was bronzed and outdoorsy-looking, well muscled (not stuffed), with a firm chin and good cheekbones much like his mother's. But he certainly looked disapproving, his dark eyes mirroring disbelief under the shock of wavy, almost black hair He transferred the look of disbelief from his mother to Jenny herself, and added a touch of suspicion. "Highway robbery. A dollhouse, I ask you."

"Bennet, don't be crass. It *is* my money, after all." Jenny suspected that all the woman needed was more of her son's disapproval and she would order a house on the spot.

"My prices are very competitive," Jenny told him coolly, "and the workmanship is perfect. And guaranteed." *Rooflines always straight,* she added to herself, and glanced again at Gillyflower Cottage.

"I should hope so." He was actually glowering at her.

Jenny put on her sweetest smile and looked back at

his mother. ''Take one of my brochures, if you'd like,'' she told her. ''You can always think about it.''

''Indeed I can. Without my son's help.'' The corners of her mouth were twitching slightly. ''My name, incidentally, is Louise Young,'' she told Jenny. ''And this is my very rude son Bennet.''

''I'm delighted to meet you both.'' Well, perhaps that was a half truth, but Jenny smiled unconsciously at the man's back as he and his mother disappeared into the crowd. He was talking nonstop, hands making emphatic gestures, and she could just imagine what he was saying.

Mother was obviously a neophyte miniaturist, and he was probably thinking Mother was obviously losing her mind, or at least her good sense. And would certainly lose her money.

''Men,'' she said eloquently to Gilda, who just smiled and shook her head. In this world of tiny details, men could be either top-notch miniaturists, like her own father, or total skeptics. Or, as was the case too often, they could simply exhibit a slightly indulgent superiority—an attitude that infuriated Jenny.

It was nearly nine when she asked Gilda to spell her for a short break. Only another hour to go, but her buzzing head called out for a jolt of caffeine, and coffee was being served in the lobby. She needed to wander for a few minutes, to breathe, to be an anonymous viewer rather than Jennifer Blakemore, mistress of Magnificent Miniature Mansions.

Her wandering netted her more than a jolt of caffeine. She was bent over the drinking fountain when the other jolt hit, causing her to jump sharply and spray water all over her glasses.

"You know, I could buy quite a nice little sports car for that amount of money." Bennet Young was leaning against the wall next to the drinking fountain, tie loosened, shirt slightly rumpled, expensive silky-looking jacket slung over his shoulder. A harried look had replaced his previous look of boredom, she saw after she quickly wiped the moisture from her glasses on the tail of her chambray shirt and was able to focus. Mother was apparently giving him a run for his money this evening.

She managed to smile, and conquered the almost overwhelming desire to kick him in the shins. "You could, of course, I'm sure," she told him as sweetly as she could. "It's all a matter of priorities, I guess, isn't it? Different toys for the boys."

He blinked. She had scored a point, she thought smugly.

"Is your mother enjoying the show?" She didn't need to ask whether *he* was.

"Too much," he said glumly. "She's getting all kinds of ideas. Although, I suppose, it's all harmless. Maybe it's even good for her. Though it certainly seems like an expensive hobby."

"So are sports cars."

He stared at her for a moment, then shrugged. "As she said, it's her money." He stirred restlessly and stood up straight, glancing down at his watch. "Where the devil is she, anyway? I offered to take her out for dinner and she had this sudden impulse to stop by here first. We won't eat until midnight at this rate."

Poor beast, Jenny thought cynically. Growling and pacing, waiting to be fed. Throw him a side of beef and he would probably settle down.

"I'm sure she'll be along soon. There's a lot to see in here." She was growing impatient with his impatience.

He shook his head at her, almost smiling for the first time. "I get grumpy when I'm hungry," he said half apologetically. "And from what I could see in here, you could spend a fortune in a very short time, carry it all home in a shoebox, and eat beans and hamburger forever after."

It was a valid observation, as she knew well from personal experience. She managed to refrain, however, from making any comment about the amount of money that could be spent on the care and feeding of a sports car.

A suspicion prickled teasingly at the edges of her mind: The man might be a bit worried about Mummy spending his inheritance on what he considered frivolous things. She knew small-minded people like that, and didn't like them much. Didn't he know that a parent who was active and full of ideas and interested in all kinds of ventures was a blessing? She thought of her father and swallowed hard.

"I'm surprised you even brought her to the show," she said before she could stop herself. She could hear the edge of hostility in her own voice.

"She brought me. I thought I explained that." He

was looking at her closely, so closely that she could feel a flush spreading across her cheekbones. She backed away a step. "Yes. Well. I have to get back to my table," she said, trying to regain her poise. "But try a little patience, Mr. Young. It takes time to absorb all the wonderful small things in life, doesn't it? But it's worth taking the time to do a thorough job of it."

"Was that a 'stop and smell the flowers' speech by any chance?" His eyes showed a glint of amusement, although he didn't actually smile. "Philosophy in miniature?"

She shrugged and pushed her glasses up her nose, studying his face silently for a moment. It was rather a nice face, and would probably be even nicer if he would allow himself to smile. "You can take it that way if you want to. I have to get back to my table. Enjoy yourself."

"I'll certainly try. See you again."

Not if I can help it, she thought as she turned from him and went back into the display room. But just when she turned away she caught a glimpse of a slight lift to the corners of his mouth. It made him look more like his mother, though all in all she much preferred the silvery Mrs. Young.

He looked after her, dark eyebrows nearly meeting over his nose in an exasperated frown. Women. Independent in unpredictable ways—even his mother. "Takes all kinds, I guess," he mumbled to himself. He should know that by now.

Funny. It almost seemed as if she had left a trail of tiny sparks of electricity in her wake. High energy, that one. Redheads were like that, sometimes. Her houses cost a lot too. Probably just another one of those women who were dead set on building up their bank accounts at the expense of others.

He gave an eloquent sigh and looked at his watch again.

The pace remained brisk for nearly all of the two-day show, and Jenny didn't have much time to think of Mrs. Young and her disapproving son. Cautious hands, admiring eyes, endless questions—and best of all, lots of sales.

Dad should be pleased, Jenny thought late Saturday afternoon when she finally had time to think. Three of his Hoosier cupboards, several tables and chests, and his dovetailed hope chests had sold well, and she had orders for more. The minutely perfect glass and ceramic accessories and original oil paintings had sold well too.

Half-finished Gillyflower Cottage was a sensation. The somewhat eccentric roofline seemed quite acceptable, even desirable. She could have sold it at least twice over, even though eyes widened at the total cost.

Still, no one reacted quite as badly as—what was his name?—Bennet Young. And Gillyflower Cottage was a display piece only, being done for a client, a mystery writer in Salem who had always wanted a thatched cottage of her own.

Gilda was tired but content too. "I'll miss some of my little people, though," she said wistfully. At an average of two hundred dollars per little person, she could afford to miss them. "Especially Toby."

"So do another Toby," Jenny told her heartlessly. Even though she admired Gilda's work, she really didn't care much for the idea of having small people wandering around her miniature rooms and houses. She preferred to have the settings all to herself. She always had a completely irrational feeling that one of the life-like little inhabitants might spill the milk, or drink all the wine, or leave shoes and dirty socks haphazardly on the bathroom floor. This was silly, she knew, but there it was. . . .

"I have four nibbles on building new houses and one confirmed contract," she said dreamily. "And I have a very strong feeling that Mrs. Young will be back in spite of her son. Or *to* spite him, as the case may be. He was a grump, wasn't he?"

"Was he?" Gilda closed her display case and glanced sideways at Jenny. "I thought he was pretty good-looking, what little I saw of him."

"Really? I didn't notice." Not quite true. "He was so busy being unpleasant."

"First impressions can be misleading but important. Anyway, your dad is going to be pleased with the construction boom. I've really missed him this show—he's one neat guy."

"Yep," Jenny said in complete agreement, her face sobering. "He had a bad cold last week. He's still fighting it. Sometimes he just doesn't seem to have much in reserve anymore. . . ."

Gilda gave her a quick hug. "Tell him hi for me, and drive carefully on the way home."

Obediently, Jenny guided her van carefully though not necessarily always within the speed limit. It was a relief to leave Boston and the bustle of the miniature show behind. She wished Dad was there to talk to. Dissecting people, discussing the things they had seen, making plans—he was good company. On his good days.

She wondered how he would have handled the skeptical Bennet Young. Strange, the way his name had stuck in her mind—almost as if she had heard it before somewhere, or had met him someplace. But she was sure she hadn't.

Anyway, Dad's way of dealing with Bennet probably would have been to lean back in his wheelchair and good-naturedly let *her* handle everything. He had been doing that more and more lately.

It was worrying, this withdrawal, and it was one compelling reason why she zipped across the Connecticut River and into the Berkshires with less regard for the speed limit than was usual for her. Home to Wellston, home to make sure Dad had done all right without her.

Her neighbor, Liz Ware, met her at the door, causing Jenny's heart to contract momentarily.

"Liz! Is Dad all right? I didn't expect you to be here!"

The good-natured eyes peering at Jenny through heavy glasses lit with the hint of a twinkle and the broad face creased into a reassuring smile. "Oh, sure, Jenny honey. We were just playing a game of gin rummy to pass the time till you got here." Liz held the door wide. "Your dad's just fine. Such a dear."

Jenny refrained from lifting an eyebrow. It was understood that Liz would check on Dad when Jenny had to be gone for any length of time. But sometimes Jenny thought Liz brought more than a neighborly zest to the job. She spoiled him terribly, but Jenny was grateful for her help.

"I'll leave now that you're here, dear." Liz followed Jenny into the comfortable kitchen where Dad sat in his wheelchair, watching the kitchen door with expectancy. "She's here, George. I'll just get my sweater and go."

"Thanks, Liz," George Blakemore said, "for bringing over the soup and for letting me beat you at gin. Jenny, you do look beat."

Liz, sweater slung over her shoulders, tarried momentarily at the back door, seeming to want to experience and absorb their thanks to the fullest. Then, with a small smile and a furtive wink at George, she was gone.

"You did all right, then, while I was away," Jenny said.

"Now, of course I did, honey. Liz came over and checked on me just the way you told her to. And you know I can get along pretty well."

"I know, but still. . . ."

He sidestepped the issue. "Tell me about the show

and the displays—did you meet new people, see new things? And I suppose you had to buy something.''

Jenny wished he wasn't forcing this interest in the show. There was a lilt missing from his voice, a glint absent from his eyes.

''Well, don't I always?'' she asked him lightly, watching his reaction closely. ''Some things I can't live without and some things I can. I bought a silver soup tureen and a walking cane and a plucked chicken.''

''A plucked chicken? You couldn't live without a plucked chicken?''

''For the kitchen of Merry Manor. You've got to admit it'll be a conversation piece.'' Merry Manor was her own dollhouse, a Victorian villa that, like many real Victorians, seemed to grow out in various unexpected directions when she had time to work on it.

There had been a number of things at the show that she could live without, though. Her mind seemed to jump of its own volition to Bennet Young's supercilious attitude. She could still see the expression in his dark hazel eyes, the crisp springiness of his almost black hair. Amazing how disagreeable people could sometimes imprint themselves indelibly on the memory, even when they would be better forgotten.

''. . . orders for any new houses?'' George was asking, and she pulled her wayward thoughts together. She told him of the confirmed contract, and of the nibbles that might turn out to be orders.

And of course that included telling him about Louise Young. She tried to gloss over—she hoped amusingly—the negative attitude Bennet had displayed. Her father smiled at her description, but watched her closely as she gave it. She changed the subject as soon as she could.

It was late before they were talked out and she helped him into bed and finished unloading the van. She finally wrestled Gillyflower Cottage onto the toolbench in their small work-room and stood studying the roofline. It was fine—just wonderful, in fact. And how could there *possibly* be people like Bennet who didn't appreciate fine miniatures?

She straightened items in the small showcase room and repositioned a few of the pieces with holding wax. All neat and tidy and perfect, she thought smugly. That night she dreamed of a misty thatched cottage, and a silvery lady leading a small boy by the hand along a flowery English garden path. He was pulling a lipstick-red toy sports car behind him and looking back at Jenny, sticking his tongue out at her in a very rude way.

"I didn't see *this* before." Bennet was peering closely at a five-inch-high William and Mary highboy that perched proudly atop the mantel. "Do you mean somebody actually painted that design on there? And with what, a brush with one hair? I didn't realize you'd brought home a souvenir of the show. It looks extremely expensive." He turned to look affectionately at his mother, who looked back at him with a hint of mischief in her eyes.

"It is called japanning, and there may have been

two hairs in the brush, and yes, it was expensive. There was a highboy much like that at Birney House long ago. I bought it when you weren't looking, dear. You really aren't very observant, you know."

He shrugged. "Overpriced dollhouses just aren't my thing." Suspicion began to dawn in his eyes. "Does this mean you're really thinking about ordering a copy of Birney House from that woman with the wild red hair and the huge glasses?"

"Well. You were more observant than I thought, after all. Her name is Jennifer Blakemore, and she has very lovely eyes and a great deal of talent, I thought. Rather attractive too. Or were you not observant enough to notice that?" Her words were even slower and more precise than usual, and she looked intently at her son, whose face remained disappointingly impassive. "I am going to give her a call, anyway. And I want you to show her around Birney House. She might have to take measurements or whatever it is she does."

"Why me?" he protested.

"Because, dear, the arthritis in my knee has been bothering me a bit, and I really don't feel up to climbing stairs. Especially those steep back stairs at Birney House. So you will do the honors, won't you, if it's necessary? After all, you aren't busy with anything else right now. You do have the time."

He made a helpless gesture with his hands and looked a little grimly at the miniature highboy. Mother was matchmaking, or at least thinking about matchmaking. She probably had surreptitiously checked the miniature maker's hand for a wedding ring—she had a habit of doing things like that. He doubted very much that her knee was bothering her. It was his bachelorhood that was bothering her, and it wasn't bothering him at all.

That and the fact that he wasn't working right now. Mother had always subscribed to the old saying that the devil finds work for idle hands to do. She tended to overlook the fact that the devil could probably guide busy hands too. Spending time exploring the corners and shadows of an old house with an electrically charged miniature maker didn't sound like much fun, but if it would make Mother happy. . . .

"All right," he mumbled in capitulation. Not very gracefully, he knew, but he couldn't see any easy way out of it. "Rotten idea, though. Waste of time." He looked hard at his mother, who stared back at him serenely with her firm chin tilted upward.

"The miniature house or the miniature maker? I think you are much too negative, Bennet. I believe you take after your Great-Uncle Harold in that respect."

"Now, Mother—"

"Hear me out, Bennet. That awful business with Cheryl was over with three years ago and should be relegated to the past. You made a mistake and almost married the wrong woman, and it's high time you got on with a normal life. Not all young women are gold diggers or—what is that term?—bimbos. Some are quite nice, very much like myself—"

A snort of laughter cut her off. "Mum, dear, nobody could be quite like you. And besides, you're rich. That does make a difference, you know."

"Of course, dear, it does make life much more pleasant. Now, I am going to call Jennifer Blakemore, and you are going to behave yourself."

His snort this time was a little more subdued. After all, Jennifer Blakemore was no more interested in him personally than he was in her.

Since "that awful business with Cheryl," he had hardly looked at a woman. He hadn't had time, for one thing. And it had been hard on the ego, after all, to be darned near left standing at the church when Cheryl decided his life-style would just never mesh with hers. She had been right, though, and he had known it. And if she hadn't backed out, he probably would have.

Morning was pure golden October, bursting with sunshine and autumn colors, and Jenny felt as if she had just crawled out from under a very heavy rock.

She squinted at the sunshine, yawned cosmically several times, massaged aching muscles where no muscles should exist, let alone ache. Her mind felt like lukewarm pasta, her brain leaping from one subject to another with all the grace and agility of an aged slug.

"Day-after hangover," Dad grunted after one glance at her. "Glad I didn't go." He didn't mean that. At least she certainly hoped he didn't—he had enjoyed the shows so much over the past three years.

"I'll survive," she grumbled. "Thanks for making the coffee."

"Figured you'd need some this morning. And there are some cinnamon rolls over there—Liz brought them yesterday morning. What's first on our agenda now that the show's over?''

''Finishing Gillyflower, of course—I promised it by Christmas. What about making some spinning wheels? And I've been thinking about a glass and tile Art Deco room just for us—if we can find the time.''

''Glad to see you're waking up at last this morning.'' George chuckled, wheeling his chair expertly toward the sink. ''On the other hand, maybe you should go back to bed for a while and let me rest.''

''Not a chance. We have work to do. And today we're going to be sure you do your exercises.''

''Bah. Liz doesn't make me do my exercises when you're not here. They don't do any good, anyway.''

Bah, indeed. Jenny squelched the tiny prickle of frustration that had become all too familiar over the past few months. Was it frustration with her dad, for giving up? Or with Liz, for encouraging him to do so?

Or was it with herself, for reasons she wasn't quite sure she wanted to admit?

Chapter Two

By late afternoon they had made plans, she had coaxed and cajoled until Dad did his exercises, and she had even had time to spend an uninterrupted hour on Gillyflower.

Well, almost uninterrupted.

Liz had brought over fresh-baked oatmeal cookies in the middle of the afternoon just after George had finished his last, and rather painful, efforts to straighten his legs and work groups of muscles that were no longer muscles. The strain showed in his eyes.

Liz sympathized with him. "I think that's too much for you. Jenny, you're a slave driver."

"He's never going to get better without it," Jenny said through gritted teeth. It wasn't easy—for her or for Dad. As good as the cookies smelled, she wished Liz hadn't come, and then immediately felt guilty for not being more appreciative.

Liz had looked contrite, sensing Jenny's reaction. She stayed only a while, and when Jenny excused herself to go work on Gillyflower, Liz nodded understandingly.

"Such a beautiful house," Liz said wistfully. "Wish I could do things like that. But cooking's my thing, I guess. I'm too clumsy for such fine little details. Well, I'd better get home and start my own dinner. It's hard cooking for one, you know. I'm not used to it."

Jenny saw Liz to the door and turned back toward George thoughtfully. "I don't think Liz likes being a widow. Better look out, Dad. I'm beginning to think—"

"Nonsense," her father snapped sharply. He swung his chair abruptly away from her and stopped beside the kitchen window, looking out at the brilliant afternoon. His shoulders slumped, and he was silent for a few long moments.

"Summer's over," he said at last, sadly. "Soon there'll be snow, and cold, and the long nights—I don't know, Jenny. I just don't know." He sighed, and she could sense that he was a long way from a vermilion autumn day, caught somehow in the cold of a winter night.

"Dad, you'll be all right. We just have to work at it."

"I'm not sure I believe that any more. What kind of life can either of us—"

The ringing of the phone cut off his sentence. Jenny crossed the room, feet dragging just a little, and picked up the wall extension.

Her jaw felt tight, and she eyed the dejected slope of her father's shoulders with concern as she answered. She would have to talk to the doctors and therapists again. . . .

The voice on the other end brought her abruptly out of that discouraging line of thought.

"Jennifer Blakemore? Oh, good. This is Louise Young, I don't suppose you remember me, but I talked to you at the miniature show. I do hope I didn't catch you at a bad time."

Jenny brought her attention back to business. That musical voice with its very precise syllables so soon? Junior must be having fits. That thought brought a small sense of triumph that made her feel just slightly better.

"Of course I remember you. You asked about a saltbox."

"What a good memory you have! I have been thinking about it ever since I saw you, and then I looked at your card and saw that you live only about twenty miles from me. I think it was meant to be, don't you? Bennet keeps reminding me that you are apparently very busy, and that I should not jump into anything, but I just had to call."

Good grief, did her son live with her? It sounded like it. At least he seemed to be within trouble-making distance.

"There's no reason why we can't at least talk it over. There certainly would be no obligation on your part," Jenny said reasonably, though she sincerely hoped that there wouldn't be a certain third party present during the talking.

"Exactly what I told Bennet. Where do we start? Should I send photos? Or would you like to come and see the house? Do we sign a contract, and how much of a deposit would you require? I know I must wait my turn, but I certainly would like to get started.''

Jenny grinned. Well. Mrs. Young might be silvery and slightly fragile in appearance, but she definitely knew her own mind—so there too, Bennet Young. In fifteen minutes she and Mrs. Young mapped out a number of details, including an invitation to Jenny to come and visit, take pictures, bring a contract, and have lunch. ''Next Saturday, then?'' Enthusiasm brought a lilt to Mrs. Young's voice. *She'll be fun to work with,* Jenny decided.

Jenny hung up the phone and leaned against the wall beside it, her mind unexpectedly filled with the vivid image of that unimaginative offspring of Mrs. Young's.

She tried to shake the vision away and looked over at George. He had turned to watch her, his shoulders square again, his chin lifted. He was fighting, thank heavens.

''Interesting call?'' he asked curiously, a hint of a smile in his eyes.

''Oh, very interesting indeed,'' she answered. ''*Very* interesting.''

On Saturday Jenny packed her camera, notebook, and portfolio into the van, started a pot of chili for Dad's lunch, asked Liz to pop in for a few minutes to check on him, and, after some serious consideration, decided to wear tailored gray slacks and a flame-colored turtleneck sweater. And good shoes for walking, if she had to count stair treads and windows and check attics.

She headed down the highway with a sense of anticipation that was tempered by niggling uncertainties. Dad was pretty self-sufficient in many ways. The house had been adapted for his special physical needs. But she couldn't adapt life for his special emotional needs, and she felt uneasy about him.

He had seemed to be doing so well up until recently, even though she had to nag him about his excercises. He was putting the memory of the accident behind him, coming to terms with Mother's death, making a new life.

But now. . . . Why could she feel this insidious, creeping depression wrapping around him like an invisible wall of frost, sometimes shutting her out entirely? Granted, his recovery was taking much too long. Still, with time he would be all right.

And there was also her wariness about just how much of a nuisance Bennet was going to be. On that score, though, she could play it cool and let his mother handle it. After all, Bennet was Mrs. Young's problem, not hers.

Tour buses full of leaf peepers shared the highway with her. It was that time of year—the best time, she thought, even though it made Dad unhappy.

She passed through Stockbridge at a crawl in what, for that town, masqueraded as gridlock, smiling at the sight of corn husks and pumpkins bedecking the porch of the Red Lion Inn. Stockbridge was a Norman Rockwell world. It was reassuring, if perhaps not quite real.

She wanted it to be real—in much the same way that she wished each of her miniature rooms and houses could be real.

She glanced down at the directions Mrs. Young had given her: three miles out of town, past the stone wall on the left, up the hill. Ignore the sign that says PRIVATE ROAD, NO ADMITTANCE, and take the gravel road past the cottage (some cottage, Jenny noted wryly, it must have at least ten rooms) and around the curve to the left.

And there it was. But it wasn't a saltbox at all, she saw with surprise, it was a large, square, stone Victorian with a mansard roof and imposing turret. Interesting. Heavy columns stood on either side of a classically arched entrance. She immediately envisioned it in miniature, which was an occupational habit, if not hazard. Everything had to be mentally reduced to an inch-to-the-foot scale. Well, most things, anyway. She clenched her jaw and adjusted her glasses on her nose.

The man standing stolidly between the pillars at the top of the short flight of entry stairs could never be imagined as six inches tall. He would never, never fit into one of her perfect houses. He was too big, too obviously alive, and in general too much. Undoubtedly, he would wreak havoc in any miniature room by merely touching it.

Scolding herself for her defensive, childish fantasy, she pulled into the graveled area at one side of the house and jumped out of her van, slinging her work satchel over her shoulder. Leaning with folded arms against one of the columns, Bennet appeared to be following her every move, like an eagle watching a field mouse.

It was necessary to take a deep breath and force what she hoped was a natural smile to her face before she turned to walk toward him. How awkward this was. It would have been so much nicer if Mrs. Young herself had been standing there.

But, to her surprise, he looked relaxed and pleasant. Apparently he wasn't going to devour her after all. She hitched her satchel more securely onto her shoulder and extended her hand as she approached him. "How do you do, Mr. Young. Nice to see you again."

His hand engulfed hers, and the warmth of it—and of his smile—took her off guard. Something apparently caught him off guard too, for he dropped her hand rather abruptly and the smile wavered for an instant. He cleared his throat and the smile returned, although the look in his eyes reminded her once again of an eagle.

"Please call me Bennet. Mother's inside and very anxious to see you and talk to you." She couldn't help but notice that he hadn't said anything about *his* being glad to see her.

And I do hope you're not going to hover over us, Jenny thought ungraciously. Maybe it wasn't the hovering that she had to worry about, but the sudden swoop downward on unsuspecting prey. *But I'm not a helpless mouse,* she thought combatively, glaring at him. He saw her expression and his eyebrows lifted slightly.

What on earth was the matter with her? She was overreacting to everything. She rearranged her thoughts and tried once again to smile naturally. But where was the saltbox she had come to see, anyway? And why wasn't Bennet off doing whatever it was that Bennet did for a living? Granted it was a Saturday, but he seemed disturbingly available to his mother's whims. Or was there the possibility that he didn't do anything for a living? Could he be one of those parasitic men who sponged off doting parents? And what business was that of hers, anyway?

There went her overreactive imagination again.

Bennet gave her the same kind of smile she had just given him and turned to lead the way into the house. Jenny humphed internally, not able to let go of her questions about Bennet's vocation—or lack of it. She followed a step behind him into the high-ceilinged entry hall.

Don't jump to conclusions, she warned herself, but she found that she was staring with righteous disapproval at his broad, able-bodied shoulders, and it took another concentrated effort to relax and find something that resembled an honest-to-goodness smile again.

Mrs. Young's materialization in the doorway at the right lifted some of the tension that hung like an invisible curtain. Jenny had to admit that she was generating most of the tension herself. *He* seemed to be on his best behavior, and the least she could do was try to follow suit.

She gave herself a mental shake. Still, she rather hoped that Bennet would tactfully disappear once he had delivered her into his mother's hands. He didn't.

She was led—with Bennet still trailing along behind,

silent as a substantial ghost—into what Mrs. Young called the morning room. The house was even bigger inside than out, some of the rooms cavernously elegant. But it definitely wasn't a saltbox. Jenny gazed around, fascinated but still puzzled.

By the time they had settled themselves into comfortable wicker-and-chintz chairs in the cheerful room, Jenny had been told that she was to call her hostess Louise, that the coffee maker on the side table held fresh coffee, that lunch would be served in the morning room at twelve-thirty, and that Louise was looking forward to working with her.

"And I with you," Jenny said, careful not to look toward Bennet. He had ensconced himself silently in a high-backed wicker chair across the room after wordlessly making sure that both women had cups of coffee. He was apparently well-trained, in some ways. He just sat there looking at them over tented fingers with a thoughtful regard that brought all Jenny's nerve endings zinging to the surface.

"Birney House is a little less than a mile up the road. It was the original house on the property," Louise said, resolving one question. "We have second cousins who live in it for most of the year, but they are on a trip to Europe right now. After lunch, Bennet will be delighted to take you there and give you a tour, so to speak. There are days," she added, only slightly apologetic, "when I do not get around as well as I would like to. . . ."

Jenny shot a quick glance at Bennet. He didn't look particularly delighted. Well. This could be an interesting day, a fascinating challenge. She began to feel a slight sense of anticipation.

"It'll be my pleasure," he commented unexpectedly, and she could swear there was a hint of amusement in his voice, as if he knew exactly what she was thinking.

She gave him her warmest, most melting smile in a deliberate effort to take him off guard, and was inordinately pleased when he blinked and looked slightly puzzled. It was one small and insignificant victory, but she had the definite feeling that, with this man, even small victories were hard to come by. He seemed the type who liked to be in control.

Their lunch was served at a small chintz and lace–covered round table beside the wide windows. Outside, grassy meadows rolled gently away to meld into copses of trees that blazed with autumn fire in the sunlight.

Louise had a cook-housekeeper, Mrs. Huckaby, a silent, plump woman with a short crop of gray hair and a bright blue apron that matched her eyes. She glanced sideways at Jenny with a certain amount of suspicion. Jenny wondered—perhaps unfairly—whether Bennet had told the housekeeper who she was and what she was doing there in such a way as to stir suspicion that Mother might be losing her marbles as well as parting with a chunk of her money.

However, from what she had seen so far, it appeared that money was not one of Louise's more pressing worries. And it was no wonder that Mrs. Huckaby was plump; the cold ham, soufflé, and fruit salad were delicious. Jenny always ate heartily when she was nervous, and she found herself devouring lunch as if she were breaking a long fast.

So what are you nervous about? she asked herself, feeling slightly ill at ease for no reason she could pinpoint. *Is the interesting challenge too much for you?*

She put down her fork and took a deep breath. This was ridiculous. Bennet had not said anything to make her feel uncomfortable or unwelcome. In fact, he had hardly said anything at all. And yet she did feel uncomfortable.

The problem was, she admitted reluctantly to herself, that she found him physically attractive. In spite of the sparks of antagonism that had flared at their first meeting, there were other sparks—ones that were definitely not antagonistic—that were struggling to kindle.

She didn't know anything about him, after all, and she didn't want to have to deal with an attraction to a man who seemed, at best, spoiled and apparently lazy and disapproving.

". . . brought home quite a few books from the county library on miniature making," Louise was saying, in perfect syllables full of wonder and charm. "I just cannot understand how I have overlooked the possibilities for so many years."

"It can be addicting," Jenny agreed, forcing herself back to the business at hand, "and very time-consuming."

Bennet ended his silence with something that Jenny could have sworn was a snort, but he quickly changed it to a slight cough. "Mom has lots of time and no other known addictions," he said softly.

"And I found a miniature shop in Abbotsford," Louise said eagerly. "I am so anxious to get started. I am going to start collecting and making things right away. Oh, I cannot wait until you have seen Birney House. It will make such a wonderful project, won't it, Bennet?"

"Mmm," Bennet answered. Jenny had never heard such an ambivalent noise.

Bennet offered to drive to Birney House. She almost said that it might be a beautiful walk, but then she realized a walk would mean more time to talk, and she didn't really know what kind of a conversation she could manage with this taciturn, vaguely disapproving man. Besides, her big satchel with notepads and camera was heavy, and so she agreed to let him drive.

It was almost disappointing that he didn't drive the little red sports car of her dream. In fact, his van was much like her own, although it looked as if it had been used recently to haul a load of questionable items to the dump. Litter. Debris. Jenny sniffed and brushed a potato chip from the front seat.

He was either disorganized or totally uncaring about anything resembling neatness. She was right: He would never fit into one of her perfect miniature worlds.

"Sorry about the mess," he said, not sounding very sorry. "I've been shifting equipment around and trying to clear out the gatehouse. Well, you know how it is. One mess always leads to another."

"Yes," she said. That had been an extremely profound statement on his part, actually. One mess does lead to another. *Go easy, Jenny, and look at this whole thing objectively—you have a job to do and that's all there is to it*, she thought.

"This shouldn't take too long," she offered, almost apologetically, although she didn't know why she should apologize. She felt sure she wasn't wasting his valuable time, since he seemed to have all the time in the world to waste.

She glanced over at him, questions bubbling through to her consciousness—questions that she knew she couldn't ask, such as just who and what are you, Bennet? What do you do for a living? Or don't you do anything? *And why do you watch me as if I were a vampire about to drain blood from your mum's neck?*

He wasn't looking at her right now, though. He stared ahead at the winding gravel road, apparently totally unaware of her glance. His dark hair and eyes gleamed with vitality. She sensed his intelligence and controlled energy.

Jenny blinked as if a blinding light had flashed across her eyes and mind and looked away, but not soon enough. His profile was still burned into her awareness: a fine nose, what she thought of as strong and aristocratic, and a jawline with the same strength. He was probably an extremely stubborn man, she told herself. Spoiled, maybe. Certainly used to getting his own way.

"Birney House is just around the curve," he said, breaking into her thoughts with a quick smile that made Jenny catch her breath in the irrational fear that he might have been reading her mind.

He brought the van to a halt at the end of a short

drive that led to one of the most gracious old saltboxes Jenny had ever seen. Every board and windowpane seemed to be in its original condition, and the surrounding junipers and boxwood and maples cradled and protected it. It looked timeless, loved, welcoming.

"Please feel free to take all the time you want," he was saying as she scrambled unceremoniously and eagerly out of the car with camera already poised. "You don't have to hurry. I have nothing else to do. I'm between jobs right now."

She almost felt that he was laughing at her. Why did he keep making her feel that she was at a disadvantage? Maybe it was that feeling—a feeling she didn't like at all—that prompted her to ask the question.

"What is it that you do when you *do* have a job, then?" She was horrified at herself as soon as she asked it, but it was out before she could stop herself. She also realized that it sounded like a challenge, but there was no way to change that now. Besides, she was genuinely curious.

But the words fell into a sudden silence between them like invisible lead weights, lying there unanswered for the space of two or three heartbeats.

In an unexpected flash of intuition, Bennet thought he understood the impression she must have of him. An unemployed scrounger who didn't want his mother spending her money—*his* inheritance—foolishly. It wasn't a very flattering picture.

She had just shot an arrow right through his pride and his first impulse was to return the shot. He opened his mouth to tell her the truth, that he was rather famous, thank you, as an award-winning documentary filmmaker. And then he realized how stuffy that would probably sound. He wasn't used to being put in the position of having to explain himself to anybody. Besides, she really should have known who he was without an explanation, shouldn't she?

It just went to prove that she wasn't as smart as those big glasses made her look. But then, answered a more logical side of his ego, not everyone in the world knows the name Bennet Young. He sighed.

Let her wonder a little. Mom would probably set her straight soon enough. Like most mothers, she liked to brag if she had a chance.

"I'm in films from time to time," he said. He unlocked the door to Birney House and waved her in.

"That's very interesting." She stepped inside and turned to look at him again, poking her glasses up on her nose and squinting at him slightly, trying to remember if she had ever seen him on either a big screen or a small one. "Then have I seen you on television? Or in a movie?"

There was a curious hesitation before he answered. "I doubt it," he finally said. "I doubt it very much."

She should have guessed something of the sort. An aspiring actor. Somehow it was disappointing.

Birney house, however, was anything but disappointing. She made notes of the general layout of the rooms, taking extensive measurements, counting stairs, getting snapshots, and trying very hard to ignore the fact that she had a shadow. Bennet dogged her footsteps wordlessly. She felt as if she were being stalked. Did he think she was going to steal a newel post?

Once she glanced around quickly at him and caught him grinning. She smiled back and asked him sweetly if the house had any ghosts.

"Why? Can you make those in miniature too? It must be hard to get measurements."

She refrained from throwing the tape measure at him. Her patience while working on miniatures was inexhaustible, her patience with difficult people and situations less so. She had been known to throw things occasionally. Dad blamed it fondly on her red hair. She took a deep breath. "Just curious. Old houses often do have a reputation for being haunted." Her camera flash briefly illuminated a fireplace wall. "And to answer your question, yes, there are a number of very well-done haunted houses in miniature."

He actually laughed. "Haunted by what—the ghosts of dolls long dead? I'd like to get *that* on film."

"Mmmmm." Awful man. Mentally, she switched him off, concentrating on scribbling a little note in her notebook about the pine plank flooring.

Her pencil stopped abruptly as a very startling thought needled the surface of her mind. *On* film, he had said. He was *in* films, wasn't he? And she was unlikely to have seen him on screen?

What if—No, it was impossible. But the unwelcome thought remained. Just what kind of movies had he been in, anyway? What if she was totally alone in an unfamiliar old house with. . . . No, it wasn't possible.

Louise's son would never be in *that* kind of movie . . . if she knew about it.

She shot a nervous sideways look at him. He had a nice build, not quite a bodybuilder type but well put together, and good face, as she had already noticed. But then you don't focus in on faces much anyway in certain types of movies. She wasn't positive, but she doubted it.

Leaning against the door frame, he was looking at her with curiosity in his eyes and something else that made her heart give a sudden leap of both apprehension and unexpected pleasure. Closing her eyes, she told herself not to be ridiculous.

"Something wrong?"

At the sound of the mild concern in his voice, her eyes flew open again. She hoped she wasn't as flushed as she felt. Darn her treacherous pale skin, anyway. Her ridiculous imagination had run away with her. But now she couldn't look directly at him.

"I'd like to check upstairs before we leave," she managed to say, glad that the tremor in her voice was hardly noticeable.

"Of course. Be careful of the stairs, now. They're pretty steep." He followed her up the narrow staircase with a slight frown. What was the matter with her, anyway? He hadn't said anything that should have caused that much reaction.

Fair-skinned people blush so obviously, he thought. And, in her case, so becomingly. Her eyes behind those silly glasses of hers had gone wide and deep, the rich hazel reflecting glints of green. It had taken him off guard.

The grace of the slim body moving up the steps ahead of him was remarkable too. Not everyone could climb steep stairs with that wonderful fluidity. He felt a strange warmth breaking through the layers of self-imposed chill and fought it.

Her auburn hair with its streaks of fiery electricity had been loose and alive at the show, but today she had it pulled back and twisted professionally into a graceful swirl at the back of her head. Only a few strands escaped, lively little tendrils that he suddenly wanted to smooth into place.

Or was it that he wanted to loosen the whole mass of it, see it fall softly to her shoulders, warm his hands in its fire? As they emerged on the small landing at the top of the stairs he had to make a conscious effort to keep his hands at his sides.

This kind of a reaction was unlike him, and not at all what he had intended. *Control, Bennet, control,* he told himself. *Remember that this whole project is ridiculous, after all.*

"How did you ever start building dollhouses, anyway?" he asked, almost defensively. "Rather an odd vocation, isn't it?"

He was calling *her* vocation odd? And with that slight emphasis on the word "odd." Odd that a grown woman would play with "dollhouses." Odder that she would build them. And odder yet that it could be considered a job.

"Odd that you should ask that, actually," she answered with what she hoped was sweet rationality. "My father, like your mother, finds miniatures quite fascinating. So we work together on them."

"Together?" He was obviously mulling over her words in his mind, trying to find the answer to his question, but it didn't seem to be there. "Your father likes to build miniatures? Full-time?" he asked as if such a thought was the next thing to inconceivable.

"Not really. But it's certainly better than doing nothing, isn't it?" She gave him a meaningful stare. "He's not able to work full-time right now."

"I see." She was pretty sure he *didn't* see, but she was content to let him try to puzzle it out. "And you live with your father, do you?" he asked.

"At the present time, yes. And you live with your mother, do you?" Jenny hadn't meant for the question to be so sarcastic, but it sounded that way, even to her own ears. But she did want to know the answer. It wouldn't tell her just what it was he did in films, but it might give her a faint clue to his character.

Chapter Three

"I live at the gatehouse. For now." He looked at her closely, reading all the suspicions in her mind. He was very tempted to tell her the truth. But the truth was that he did live in the gatehouse. For now. Inwardly amused, he decided it would be interesting just to string her along. For now.

"I stay there," he added, "when I'm not working. Mother prefers not to have me underfoot all the time. She's become rather used to having the house to herself since my father died five years ago, and I sometimes get in the way. Though she's fond of me, of course."

"Of course." She turned from him with a thoughtful frown knitting her eyebrows, and he trailed behind her into the big upstairs bedroom, not quite hiding a mischievous smile.

Jenny stood silent for a moment, studying the low-ceilinged room, taking in the antique furnishings and the handsome fireplace that boasted a gloomy, primitive portrait over the mantel that watched them sternly.

"I can understand that," she added at last. He wasn't sure whether she could understand that his mother didn't want him underfoot, or that she was fond of him.

"Here, hold this while I measure the width of the fireplace," she told him before he could sort it out. She handed him the spring-loaded tape measure and their fingers brushed.

Acutely aware of the slight contact—it had felt like a tiny lightning bolt—Jenny backed away, eyes fixed determinedly on the lengthening tape.

"Is this much accuracy really necessary?" For some reason, his amusement had faded, to be replaced with wariness. "I mean, after all, it's only a toy, isn't it?"

"Only a toy!" She glared at him, almost dropping the tape. "It will be a miniature re-creation of a house that's important to your mother. Not just a 'toy.' If I wanted to make a toy I'd pound a half-dozen pieces of plywood together and cut a door in the front and spray it with some cheap paint!"

"Hey, I'm sorry." He backed off, still holding the end of the tape. "I didn't realize you were so sensitive about the whole thing."

Her glare turned into a fierce glower. "I'm not sensitive, and stand still, darn it. You're throwing off the measurements."

"Heaven forbid," he snapped, but he stood still. Measurements, measurements. Still, considering the price she was charging for this house, he supposed it really should be as accurate as possible.

He grumbled under his breath and watched her making notes and measuring and taking all of this so seriously—and she was worth watching. She had a natural grace about her. He brought his mind back sharply from its pleasant wanderings. There had to be a limit to all this finicky work. The next thing he knew she would be measuring the width of the floorboards.

She made a brief note on her pad of paper and let the tape measure snap nearly back into its casing, and then bent and measured a floorboard. He closed his eyes and wondered how long it would take her to drive him out of his mind. Not long, he suspected. He was probably already on his way.

She stood and faced him, eyes sparkling with a gleam of impishness behind those glasses. "Just making sure," she said. "I was pretty certain about the width of the flooring. Interesting, it's chestnut up here, did you know that? These small details make a world of difference."

Bennet stifled a groan. But her words registered in his rational consciousness like the refrain of some old familiar tune. *Small details make a world of difference*. Didn't he embrace that concept in every film he made? Wasn't it partly the reason for his success?

He looked at her with the reluctant beginnings of respect. Perhaps there was more to this miniature making than he had thought, although his type of attention to detail was on a much higher aesthetic level than hers. Wasn't it?

"You're right, of course," he admitted finally. "Measure on, MacDuff."

She looked surprised, and aimed an uncertain smile at him. What a face, he thought. What a wonderful face. Every emotion registered on it so guilelessly, so openly. But women, he reminded himself, were rarely guileless. As he knew only too well.

She made another note in her notebook and treated him to a repeat of that peculiarly appealing half smile, rubbing the back of her neck with her free hand and flexing her shoulders. It took a measure of self-control to keep him from reaching out to help her loosen up those tight muscles.

"Fine old saltboxes have so much character," she said almost inaudibly. He was watching her with such a strange look that she felt uneasy. He had an unnerving trick of doing that. She found it difficult to look directly into those penetrating eyes, so she switched her gaze to the portrait on the fireplace wall.

"Interesting old gentleman," she remarked in a voice that sounded much too bright to her own ears, an obvious attempt at lightness that she really didn't feel. "An ancestor of yours? I can almost see a family resemblance."

"Enoch? Enoch Hayes. Old reprobate, if family stories are right. And yes, he was a great uncle of some kind, way back there somewhere."

"Reprobate? He looks so staunch and proper."

"Is that what I look like? Staunch and proper?"

"I didn't mean it that way."

"I know." He was deliberately giving her a bad time, and nearly felt sorry for her momentarily—but not sorry enough to fight off the mischievous bubble that rose teasingly to the surface of his mind. "He was known as something of a canoodler, actually."

"Canoodler?"

"Canoodler," he repeated firmly, managing to keep a straight face. "Though he may not have used that exact word. He was anything but staunch and proper, according to the family stories."

Jenny brushed a stray wisp of hair off her forehead and shouldered her satchel, nibbling on her lower lip. Maybe, just maybe, more than a slight resemblance in appearance had come down through the family. . . .

Suddenly, she was acutely aware that she was in an unfamiliar bedroom with a man she knew practically nothing about, and who might do just about anything and everything for a living. She managed to lift her chin and look him straight in the eye, feeling like David challenging Goliath.

"I imagine," she told him as evenly as she could, "that your mother is waiting for us. I have about all the information I need right now. If I can just get a few snapshots of the exterior I think we can go back."

Her suddenly businesslike manner surprised him a little. He was used to being the one who issued directions. She certainly was unpredictable. Yet, in her case, the mood changes were challenging. He wanted to tickle and tease into the layers of that personality, see what made her tick, see what kind of reactions he could get from her.

"You're sure you have everything you want? There's nothing else you need?" His eyes seemed to look right through her.

"Not this trip. And I'll try not to bother you again." It was an effort to maintain that crisp approach when the man was communicating with her on so many different levels. Or was it just her imagination?

"Thank you for showing me Birney House, Bennet. You were very patient."

He realized it was the first time that she had used his name. The way she said it made a tiny frisson of pleasure lift the fine hairs at the back of his neck.

Watch it, Bennet, he told himself. "The pleasure was mine," he said and realized that he meant it.

At the front door, Jenny paused, looking back. She thought she had heard something, a creaking stair, a door with a rusty hinge closing slowly. But of course not. The old house was settling, adjusting itself to changing temperatures as old houses do. It was a wonderful place. Dad liked saltboxes. Maybe re-creating this one would give him a lift. She hoped so.

"You have been gone for quite awhile. I hope you got everything you needed? Was he good? Heavens, your glasses are certainly steamed up."

Louise's question pulled Jenny abruptly back to awareness of the morning room and the cup of tea steaming fragrantly in front of her. She had been watching Bennet's back as he swung easily into his van and drove back, presumably, to the gatehouse.

Was he good? The question momentarily unnerved her. Good at what, canoodling? Surely Louise didn't mean—of course she didn't.

Jenny removed her steamy glasses and laid them very carefully on the table. The foggy lenses, of course, had been caused by the tendrils of steam arising from the tea. She smiled at Louise and thought she saw a glint of mischief in the older woman's eyes.

"He can sometimes be a little edgy, especially when he is busy hatching a new project," Louise added. "Mothers just cannot help hoping that their sons will behave themselves in a courteous manner, even when they are grown men. It's part of a mother's job."

"He was very helpful," Jenny told her. "And it's a wonderful old house." She wanted to ask what kind of a new job Bennet might be hatching, but before she could decide how to phrase the question without sounding too inquisitive, Louise had seized on her last sentence and was off on an eager description of the history of Birney House and her ideas for the replica of it.

Jenny put her glasses back on and made notes and suggestions, thoroughly enjoying the remainder of her visit. She hardly even thought of Bennet for the next hour, and left with a signed contract, an eagerness to start cutting into a fresh stack of plywood, and the warm feeling that she had made a fascinating new friend.

Maybe, she told herself as she waved good-bye to Louise, *if I hurry with Gillyflower, I can get started on this sooner instead of later. If I can just light a fire under Dad, we can build the shell. If everything goes well. . . .*

When she passed the sprawling stone gatehouse, Bennet was out in front throwing a ball for a large, shaggy dog of mixed ancestry. He paused to wave at her and the dog gave a friendly bark and watched her pass with alert eyes and ears. Both of them stared after her as she drove through the gates and around the tree-shrouded bend of the road.

Idly, she wondered if throwing a ball for a somewhat ungainly dog was the way Bennet hatched new projects. It didn't seem likely, but then what did she know? In his line of work, anything was possible.

Dad was still in a gloomy blue funk when she got home. He was watching an old movie on TV, but she didn't think his mind was on it. On a better day, he would have been at the workbench, cutting and smoothing small pieces of wood or building a five-inch trellis and talking of training roses on it, or going through stacks of catalogs looking for elusive miniature supplies.

He seemed distracted and moody lately. Was he giving up on the idea of a full recovery? He couldn't give up. She wouldn't let him give up.

"Did you do your exercises today?" she asked him brightly.

He shook his head slightly, not looking at her. "Not today."

She went to his side and rested a hand lightly on his shoulder, the mixture of worry and frustration gnawing painfully at her heart. "Bad day?" she asked, uneasiness showing in her voice.

"Aren't they all?" An edge of bitterness etched his quiet reply, and she didn't like the sound of it. Then he pulled himself together and looked up at her, forcing a smile. "How did it go?"

"It's a wonderful old house. We'll love doing it."

"Will we?"

"Dad—"

"I know. I'm sorry. It's this time of year. . . ."

The accident had been in October. He didn't need to put it in exact words. She pulled the footstool over and sat down beside him, trying desperately to make eye contact, to make soul contact. But he avoided her gaze.

"Dad, it's been hard, I know. But it's been three years since the accident. And the doctors say you could still make progress. Won't you try? Won't you try to put the bad times behind you?"

"And just how can I put it behind me, sitting in this contraption all day, every day, knowing that I've taken you away from the work you were doing? How can I forget about it when it's part of my life every day, when I miss your mother every moment of every hour?"

He clamped his jaw shut, taking a deep, ragged breath. "Oh, Jenny. Forgive me. Tell me all about Birney House. We're going to have to get busy, aren't we? The two of us?"

Jenny hesitated briefly. Her father's outburst had been unusual, but she had felt it building inside him for weeks now. He was feeling guilty about being dependent on her, getting discouraged, thinking too much of the past.

She wanted to talk to him seriously to console, to encourage, and somehow to make things better. She felt like a parent instead of a child, and she doubted if she had the wisdom and patience and time to really help. But maybe the best way to do that, right now, was to talk to him about Birney House, and to try to rekindle some of his enthusiasm.

And so she told him about the saltbox, and about Louise, and even about Bennet and her curiosity about him. Though not quite *everything* about her curiosity. . . .

"Attractive man, is he?" George's voice was carefully neutral and his quick glance at her gave nothing away, but she knew—or thought she knew—what he was thinking.

"Some women would probably think so, I suppose. He seems a little, I don't know, closed in, I guess. Secretive. Suspicious."

"Sounds like a prime candidate for the C.I.A. Either that or he's some kind of skulking paranoid."

"Well, no. Not quite like that. I think he dislikes the idea of his mother spending her money on what he considers a 'toy.'"

"Aha. And the man has no visible means of support. It's interesting. Dangerous, maybe."

"Oh, come on, Dad. I promise to keep my distance, if that's what you're worried about."

"Mmmm." He shifted in his wheelchair, considering. "And are we going to be doing some of the furniture for Birney House too?"

"Probably. They still have some of the original pieces that we can copy."

"Good." He sounded brisk, more like himself. "In that case, you may have to go back to get more photos. It's nice that it's not too far away."

She agreed, but thought about it seriously as she fixed dinner and later cleared away the dishes. Bennet was a puzzle, all right, interesting and maybe dangerous, as Dad had pointed out. All of which made Jenny very curious in spite of herself.

But she didn't have time for puzzles of that sort. She had her hands full taking care of Dad. One of these days he would make that final step toward recovery. Then maybe she could take the time to try to decipher puzzles and challenges.

With determination, she put Bennet out of her mind. She didn't want to analyze the strange minnows of feeling that were swimming around just under the surface of her consciousness.

Her sleep was uneasy that night, and literally haunted by fuzzy-edged dreams. She was running through a miniature saltbox, chased by Bennet, who was holding out a metal tape measure and telling her he wanted to see how she measured up. Then a sinister, cadaverous ghost of an old gentleman stepped out of a portrait and drifted rather creakily across the floor, shouting something she couldn't quite hear.

She awoke abruptly at the edge of a scream and was weak with relief at seeing the wonderful normalcy of slanting sunrays patterning her walls. It took her a few minutes to leave the dreams behind. They clung, still vivid, at the edge of consciousness. Did old Enoch haunt Birney House the way he had haunted her dreams? Of course he wasn't the only one who had haunted last night's dreams.

"I measure up just fine, thank you," she muttered

under her breath impatiently. She got up and quickly slipped under the shower to wash away any nightmare residue and went down to put on a commonsense pot of coffee. But she couldn't quite rid herself of the dream faces of both Enoch and his descendant.

An interesting idea was forming in her mind. Connie Southwell did the tiny oil paintings that Jenny took to the shows; she was great at copying portraits. Jenny made up her mind to call Louise and ask her if she would like a scale duplicate of the painting.

By the time she had finished her second cup of coffee and settled Dad at the workbench (he was grimly determined to make up for his gloominess of the evening before), she was sure it was a marvelous idea. Even if it meant another trip to Birney House and Bennet's company.

She called right after breakfast. Mrs. Huckaby answered, sounding as if she had just been interrupted in the midst of the perfect soufflé. Jenny found herself apologizing for calling at all, then caught herself and asked somewhat imperiously for Louise. She wasn't going to be intimidated both by Bennet and the stern-faced housekeeper.

Louise was enthusiastic about the idea of copying Enoch Hayes's portrait. "You must come and get a good photograph of it. Or I can have Bennet do it—he's so good at that sort of thing. He can bring it down on one of his trips that way. What did you say Bennet called him? An old reprobate?"

Jenny really hadn't meant to say anything about Bennet's irreverent comments about his ancestor. It had just slipped out. But at least she hadn't called him a canoodler. "Oh, it was just that Enoch Hayes had something of a reputation."

"Indeed he did. He was a pillar of the community, a deacon of his church, an overseer of county records, he raised six children of his own and provided a home, it is said, for a dozen local orphans. He is a legend in our family."

Jenny gulped. This was the cadaverous ghost who had haunted her dreams last night? "He sounds as if he was a very admirable man," she managed, which was more than she could say for a many-times great nephew.

Louise chuckled. "I think Bennet was pulling your leg just a bit. He does that sometimes." She sounded pleased about it.

And just why, Jenny asked herself angrily a dozen times during that day, did Bennet feed her that silly story about Enoch Hayes? And why, come to that, did Louise sound as if that fact pleased her? She did her best to put it out of her mind.

Bennet glanced down at the envelope that lay on the seat beside him and made a face at it. Making the face didn't change a thing, but it did make him feel a little better—or did it just make him feel childish? He grinned and concentrated on the highway.

"There is no good reason, dear, why you should not deliver the photos yourself if you are going down to talk to Joe Hayes," his mother had said. "Wellston is only a few miles farther, and then Jenny can get the pictures to that painter friend of hers."

"Mommy dearest, you could always hop into your little MG and deliver the pictures yourself. Or use the U.S. mail." She gave him her sweet, wide-eyed, and stubborn look and he almost laughed. "You," he told her, "are a conniving, underhanded, devious manipulator, you know that? I know what you're up to, and you should be ashamed of yourself."

"Why, thank you, Bennet. But I am not ashamed at all."

The two of them looked at each other with identical half smiles of shared understanding for a moment, the family resemblance striking.

"So just why," Louise asked, breaking the silence, "did you tell poor Jenny that Enoch Hayes was an old reprobate? He is undoubtedly whirling in his grave. I remember when you used to tease the little girls in kindergarden with silly statements like that. And the girls in fifth grade, and junior high, and high school. . . ."

"Your memory is atrocious."

"Accurate, you mean. You always did that sort of thing to the girls you liked best. Remember?"

He remembered, and she was right. She almost always was. He really didn't want to explore his motives for regaling Jenny with an ancestral tall tale; it had been a good idea at the time. It really didn't mean a thing.

"I think," Louise said, "that you must find Jenny

Blakemore a very attractive young woman. Which she is."

"You're making something out of nothing, Mother."

"Oh, but I am right, Bennet. You are not to argue with me."

"Yes, ma'am," he said with mock humility. She laughed and looked pleased.

He wished she looked less sure of herself. It made him feel uneasy, given her record of accuracy.

Jenny had said when he called that Calder Way was just off Main Street, the second house from the corner, with a white picket fence in front. The town had many white fences and broad lawns and a sense of timelessness. Given other circumstances, he would have let the peace of the village flow through him.

But at the center of the peacefulness was a bright-eyed, titian-haired woman who did something uncanny to his hard-won sense of security and independence. He just couldn't afford in any sense of the word to let another dollar-hungry schemer into his life, or his mother's. Yet Jenny was so appealing. . . .

He pulled up to the curb in front and sat quietly for a few moments, marshaling his thoughts. He was a little early. He had told Jenny that he would be here around noon, and it was just eleven-forty. But he had gotten quick answers to his phone calls that morning, and the new project was going well. It would be good, maybe even great.

But now he had to deal with details of his mother's new project, which at this moment loomed like a thundercloud over the months of filming that lay ahead. Or maybe it was the miniature maker that sent out the storm warnings.

He would *not* tease. He would leave the photos and then drive away from Wellston, and from here on out his mother could handle all the silly little details of building a miniature Birney House. He had more important things to do.

Envelope in hand and shoulders squared, he approached the front door with a sense of purpose and rapped sharply on the front door. It was opened almost immediately, but not by Jenny, as he had expected. A man in a wheelchair with graying hair and shrewd eyes very similar to Jenny's was looking up at him, assessing him, making him feel as if he were on trial. Or as if he were a callow sixteen-year-old, calling on his first date.

"Are you Bennet Young, or are you selling something? If you're selling something, we don't need it. If you're Bennet, Jenny's out in the workshop, and you're early. By the way, I'm her father."

"Sorry." Bennet felt absurdly apologetic. "I can come back a little later, Mr. Blakemore."

"Don't be a darned fool." Jenny's father wheeled his chair expertly out of the way, a smile taking any sting out of the words. "Come on in. And please call me George." He put his hand out and Bennet shook it. The older man had a surprisingly strong grip and Bennet looked more closely at him. He had a rather abrupt way of speaking and an elusive air of sadness that was revealed by a downturn at the corners of the mouth.

"I'm glad to meet you, George." He remembered that Jenny had said her father hadn't been able to work for some time. Now he knew why.

"Go through the kitchen to the side door," George was saying. "We've set up the workshop out there. Just go on through. She's expecting you."

Bennet did as he was told. But she obviously wasn't expecting him, at least not at that exact moment. Oblivious to his quiet opening of the door, she stood with her back to him, guiding the blade of a small table saw through a thin sheet of wood and humming to herself. He was vaguely aware of a multitude of shelves and improbably neat compartments for supplies, of miniature houses in various stages of construction, and an overall feeling of order and organization.

But most of all he was aware of Jenny herself.

She reached to switch off the saw and examined the tiny piece of wood she had just cut, still humming softly. Her body swayed slightly to the music, graceful and dreamy.

Bennet stood entranced, silent. She was so wonderfully feminine, even in an oversize cotton shirt hanging loosely over well-worn jeans. He caught a glimpse of her gracefully curved neck and throat above the frame of the shirt collar, and her hair looked as if it had been caught against its will in a reluctantly confined braid that moved, caressingly alive, between her shoulder blades.

Control, he told himself. *Self-control.*

He opened his mouth to speak, to break this dangerous spell, to let her know he was there, just as her soft humming turned to words. He recognized them with a jolt of surprise: ". . . in the moonlit garden, the rosemary remembers. . . ."

" 'The Sleeping Garden,' " he said softly, involuntarily. It was a very old, obscure folk tune from Wales, a song that had barely survived into the modern world.

Startled, she jumped and turned toward him, the song dying. His unexpected appearance had obviously taken her off guard, and the color drained from her face and then flooded back.

"You surprised me," she managed. "I didn't hear you come in." Then his words registered. "You recognized it!" she marveled. "Amazing. It's not exactly a top-forty platinum favorite." Not the sort of song, her tone implied, that a clod like Bennet would be likely to recognize.

"Of course I recognized it." He said it loftily, answering her implied criticism of his taste. "You underestimate me."

"Is that possible? Oops, sorry. Just joking. I would never underestimate you."

"I'm glad to hear it. It'll make things much easier."

"For you or for me?" she asked with intense interest. The look in her eyes almost nailed him to the wall.

"For us, maybe."

"Maybe. Odd thing, though—haven't you noticed that when things become too easy they seem to lose their value?"

There were undercurrents growing in this conversation that made those storm warnings flash like lightning bolts. His nerve endings were almost vibrating. It looked as if she was just as aware of those charged currents as he was. And her reactions were feeding his. This had to stop.

"I think we should start over," she was saying reasonably. "I suppose you brought the photos of the canoodling gentleman with you? Incidentally, your mother told me the truth about him."

"Oh well. It was just a joke." It sounded pretty lame, so he just shut up and handed her the envelope without looking directly at her.

The sooner he could get out of here, the better.

Chapter Four

Jenny took the envelope from him, her fingers brushing his hand lightly. "I doubt if old Enoch would be laughing very hard," she murmured.

Bennet managed to raise his eyes to hers. "Not after all these years," he acknowledged. "But I hope the pictures will be sharp enough for your painter friend, and I'm sorry if I startled you when I came in." It was a chilly, formal apology with as much warmth as an advancing glacier.

"It's okay. Thank you for bringing them, and I'll get them to Connie right away." She looked puzzled, and did he see a touch of hurt? No doubt by now she was convinced he was some kind of nut case, a pathological liar, and a shiftless leech.

His pride was stung. He wasn't used to being thought of as a weirdo, though, in honesty, he had brought this on himself. Well, enough. He had apologized, and now it was time to get out of here. Right now. But his feet wouldn't move.

Crossing his arms, he leaned—he hoped casually—against the wall. Maybe he should try to pour a dollop of oil onto the troubled waters, which had been stirred up and muddied simply because he found her so attractive.

Teasing and distorting the truth (he hated to call it lying) and stringing her along about what he did for a living gave him a certain perverse pleasure, but it really wasn't very nice. He could almost hear his mother's voice: "Now, Bennet, you must make more of an effort to be gentlemanly. . . ."

"You know," he said tentatively, "you have a very pleasant voice. I'd like to hear all of your version of that song some day." It happened to be true, and Jenny looked at him with a glint of wary surprise.

"Thank you. I love old folk songs."

"So do I. And old gardens. Let's go somewhere for lunch."

"Lunch?"

"Midday meal. Sandwich or something. You know."

"I know what a lunch is." Jenny looked more puzzled than ever, and he didn't blame her. His spontaneous invitation had surprised him too, but now that he had said it, it sounded like a good idea. This must have been what he intended to do all along. He straightened up and smiled at her, not feeling the need for the support of the wall any more.

The smile and his sudden friendliness apparently disarmed her. The wariness and the surprise in her eyes deepened, and she backed away a step or two. "Oh, I was going to fix sandwiches for Dad and myself," she hedged. "Maybe some other time—"

''I can fix my own sandwich perfectly well,'' a voice said from the doorway. ''You run along. You need a break.'' George had wheeled himself silently to the workshop doorway, and was watching them with an amused expression.

Jenny was outnumbered, and the tiny sparks of rebellion in her eyes were magnified by her oversize glasses. ''Well.'' She looked at both of them, then down at herself. ''Thank you very much, but these are work clothes. I'm grubby and I'm—''

''Hungry, I hope,'' Bennet interrupted. He privately thought her work clothes were as attractive as sequins and silk. The smear of dust across one cheekbone added to her gamine attractiveness, and he wanted to reach out and rub it off. He clenched his hands. Be sensible, he told himself. Not just gentlemanly, but sensible.

So, sensibly, he suggested that they go to the Mill Pond Grill for one of their super burgers, since it was a casual kind of place, and he would wait while she washed up, no hurry. . . .

And, sensibly, he managed to make small talk with her father as she fled up the stairs in reluctant defeat, wondering why, in the name of all that was sensible, he had asked her to go out to lunch with him.

But he knew the answer to that. She was lovely, she was challenging, and she tugged at his masculine ego in a way that no woman had done for a long time.

And she knew ''The Sleeping Garden.''

* * *

Jenny settled back in the front seat of Bennet's van and took a deep breath, then another, staring fixedly at the road ahead.

She wished she could sort out her tangled reactions. Bennet was attractive. Very attractive. But she couldn't quite figure him out, and she had her hands full with Dad. Just what was she getting into? The whirlwind of contradictory thoughts got her nowhere.

"A penny for your thoughts."

"A penny doesn't go very far these days." Just like her thoughts, really. She paused, looking down at her hands. Couldn't she just accept this as a casual social situation, or at least try to? "I was thinking about Dad," she said softly.

"He'll be all right without you for a while."

Jenny glanced over at him quickly. "I hope so."

"Has he been—incapacitated—long?" he asked after a moment.

"About three years. There was a car accident. A drunk driver drifted over to the wrong side of the road. My mother was killed, and Dad was badly injured. I came home to take care of him until he could get on his feet, but it hasn't happened."

Her voice fell on the last words. He felt a tingle of deep sympathy for her. She had a disarming way of making him admire her and like her, and that sort of thing knocked unexpected holes in the defensive walls he had built around himself.

"I'm sorry. I didn't mean to be nosy. Will he improve?"

"I don't know. I hope so. The doctors have said that it's largely up to him now. It was all going better a few months ago, actually, but he isn't fighting back the way he should. So I stay, and I worry about him."

"I understand." He wondered if he understood more than she was telling him, wondered if perhaps her father had grown dependent on her and didn't want to let her go. But that was an uncharitable thought. "You said you came home to take care of him. Where were you living? What did your father do before he was injured? What did *you* do before he was injured, or were you building dollhouses back then too?"

"My, you really are nosy, aren't you?" She didn't sound upset about it, just a little amused. "I had a partnership in a gift shop outside Boston, and Dad ran a fleet of fishing boats and was very active. What else would you like to know?"

Lots of things, he told himself, but that would have to come later. He pulled the van into a parking space outside the grill. "Come on. I'm starved."

During the next half hour or so all his questions were put on hold, anyway. To his delight, Jenny tackled a cheeseburger as if she were breaking a month's fast. Watching her, he smiled. Cheryl had always been finicky about her food, mentally counting calories and grams of fat, coolly contemptuous of anything as common as a burger. His smile faded. He didn't want to think of Cheryl.

"Incidentally, Mother sends her regards," he said when the conversation picked up once again.

"And take mine back to her," Jenny said promptly.

"I like your mother. I love the way she talks, each word so perfectly formed."

He chuckled. "It drives me nuts sometimes. She used to try to get me to talk like that, but it was a lost cause, naturally. Mother was raised in an extremely well-to-do family. She had an English nanny when she was a child. 'I was taught,' she'd tell me, 'that little words are like little people. Each deserves all the care and attention that one can give it so that it will become well-rounded and civilized.'"

Jenny's eyes brimmed with laughter behind her huge glasses. "That's wonderful. And you sounded just like her!"

There was a tiny smear of catsup at the left corner of her soft, lovely mouth, which turned up so sweetly at the corners when she was amused. He wanted to reach out and gently rub away the catsup, run his fingers along the lovely curve of her cheek.

Or he could kiss the catsup away. . . .

No, he told himself roughly. *No way. No involvement. No. Remember what it was like with Cheryl. Remember the long months of travel and work you have ahead of you. No woman could put up with your peripatetic ways, rushing from one side of the world to the other. Remember. . . .*

He signaled the waitress for more coffee and settled back in the chrome-and-black chair and made himself look dispassionately across at Jenny. She was watching him curiously, wary once again. Some of his thoughts must have shown in his face.

"There are things you should know, I suppose, about

Mother,'' he told her. His shoulder muscles and his voice felt tight. This was going to be a *defensive* speech, and Jenny undoubtedly was going to find it *offensive*.

One part of his heart and mind wanted to put a stop to what he was about to say, but something irrationally stubborn, past pains that had seared into his soul, made him plunge ahead. ''For one thing, she's much too trusting.''

Jenny looked baffled. ''I wouldn't have thought that,'' she said after a moment. ''She seems very sensible and sure of herself. What are you trying to say?''

He ignored the question. ''After Dad died,'' he said, ''she sold our home in Boston, and was thoroughly cheated by an unscrupulous real-estate dealer. Mother had never had to deal with business matters. She still isn't very good at it. And her attorneys weren't keeping a close enough eye on things.''

''I'm sorry to hear that.'' Any hint of laughter was long gone from Jenny's eyes. They were narrowed now, watching him.

''And then, when she disposed of some of the family furnishings, she let some things go far too cheaply. 'It is all just old Victorian bric-a-brac, dear,' she said. The dealer who bought all that old bric-a-brac no doubt smiled all the way to the bank. Even Mrs. Huckaby suspected there was something shady going on, but Mother couldn't believe it.''

''A shame,'' Jenny murmured. Her hand had tightened around the handle of her coffee mug and her jaw was set hard.

''And then,'' he went on, determined to get his point

across, "she took on a 'companion' for a few months not long after Dad's death. I was gone at the time, and mother was lonely. The companion and three of Mother's diamond rings disappeared overnight and have never been seen since. She's had enough trouble, and I don't ever want her to be cheated again."

"Look, I'm sorry. But why are you telling me all this? Why is it so important? It really sounds as if you think I'm a first cousin to the real-estate agent and the 'companion.' Did you ask me to have lunch with you so you could insult me?" The fingers holding the mug were now white, and he wondered briefly if she was likely to fling it at him. Her red hair was sizzling with electricity. "Surely you don't think I'm out to steal from your mother!"

"I just want you to know the situation. You can understand why I tend to be skeptical about some of her business ventures. If I seemed hesitant about letting her get into another expensive commitment it was just that I wanted to be sure she wouldn't get stung."

He smiled, trying to soften his words, almost hating himself for what he was saying. He had wanted to say all these things when his mother first got interested in this project, and they didn't seem valid at all now that he knew more about Jenny and her father.

But his speech did push her away, put her at a distance, and that might be a good idea. It was a truthful explanation, but for the sake of his peace of mind he couldn't allow himself to feel some of the things he was feeling about Jenny.

Seeing the look on her face, he was about to add,

in spite of himself, that he was no longer worried about Jenny's motives. The heck with his peace of mind. He was acting like a self-important grouch and he was hurting Jenny and he didn't really want to do that.

But her voice sizzled across the table at him with an intensity that silenced him before he could start.

"And you feel that the price I quoted for Birney House was exorbitant and you think she's about to be taken to the cleaners again. You're despicable, Bennet. I work hard for my money, but maybe working hard is something you don't know anything about. I like your mother, and I think you're being far too protective of her. I like Birney House. But I don't much like you."

She rose quickly, staring down at him with fire in her eyes. "I think it would be a very good idea if you took me home," she said.

Well, he'd made his point, all right. And he felt miserable. He would pick a better time and try to apologize. Maybe. After all, she didn't much like him.

George sat quietly, staring blindly out the window after Jenny and Bennet left for what seemed a very long time. Guilt, pain, and despair clutched at his mind, heart, and body in equal measures. The bright torch of the maple tree in the front yard, its vivid leaves dancing in a light breeze, was a rebuke to him, as if the gray feeling that cut clear to his bones should disappear, should fade, so that he could be alive once again and get on with his life. So that Jenny could get on with hers.

He hated being helpless. He would really be better

off dead. He tried to banish that thought from his mind. But recently, he had felt worse than ever. Last autumn, even the autumn before that, he still had held hopes for recovery. But now he couldn't admit aloud, even to Jenny, how weak and unwell he felt.

Was it his own fault? Did he just want to hold on to Jenny, to keep her from leaving? The headaches, the weakness in his muscles, the vague feelings of illness, were they all psychological? The doctors had said he should be recuperating by now, but he wasn't.

Jenny had put her whole life on hold just to take care of him. That nice-looking young man she had gone out for lunch with—once he would have watched them leave with paternal approval, hoping that perhaps something would come of it.

But now, no. He couldn't think that way. He would just have to make more of an effort. . . .

He dozed in his chair, retreating into an uneasy trancelike state where he wouldn't have to think, to feel the pain, to try to understand the incomprehensible.

It couldn't have been more than ten minutes later that he heard the tap at the door, the cheerful "Hi." It was Liz. Thank goodness for Liz. She made no demands on him, and her unfailing good cheer made him feel marginally better.

"Come on in," he called. "It's unlatched."

"I saw Jenny leave," she said, bustling into the room with a foil-covered platter in her hands. "Out for lunch with a new boyfriend?"

"Just a client. The son of a client, anyway. Now,

what have you brought over this time? You really shouldn't have."

"Oh," she said modestly, "I knew it was lunchtime when Jenny left, and I didn't want you to have to bother to fix yourself something. I was making tuna sandwiches anyway, so I just thought. . . ." She beamed at him.

"Wonderful," George said. His head didn't hurt as much now that Liz was here. "And if you have the time, maybe we can play some gin rummy this afternoon."

"Wouldn't want to keep you from your miniature making, George. Next thing I know, Jenny will be mad at me."

"Don't worry about that. I can handle Jenny."

Liz smiled at him. "She's a wonderful daughter. Eat up, now."

Jenny was increasingly pleased with Gillyflower. The detail work, which was always time-consuming but so very important, was coming along well. And Dad had tried during the last week to help out more, although she couldn't help but feel that some of his enthusiasm was forced.

He hadn't even made any comments about the way she had flung herself back into the house after her lunch with Bennet, nor the fact that she had been silent and short-tempered for the rest of the day. But Dad had watched her closely in a way that made her feel uncomfortable.

Still, by the next day she had convinced herself that telling Bennet off wasn't such a terrible thing. Maybe she wouldn't have to deal with him any longer.

On Thursday morning Connie Southwell called to tell her that the miniature portrait of Enoch Hayes was finished.

"The paint's dry," Connie said. She worked in oils with infinitesimal brushes. "At least it's transportable. Want me to drop it by, or do you want to pick it up? He looks as if he was an interesting old gentleman, incidentally."

"Oh, he was," Jenny answered wryly, "or so I'm told. Let me give Louise a call. If she's not busy this afternoon, I can pick it up and run it over to her. I need to get out for an hour or so, anyway. I know she'll be anxious to see it, and you're right on the way."

"Okay. You might see if she'd like to have Mrs. Old Gentleman done too. He looks as if he needs a companion—sort of an *American Gothic* thing."

"You know, I didn't see a Mrs. Hayes. I'll see what I can find out."

She assumed that either Mrs. Huckaby or Louise would answer the phone, so she was jolted when she heard Bennet's smooth voice say, "Young residence." Maybe he was pretending to be a butler, but there was no mistake: That pleasant, deep voice was definitely Bennet's.

"This is Jenny Blakemore," she said in a business like voice, or at least she hoped it was businesslike. It was awkward talking with Bennet after their last encounter. What was she supposed to say now? Something like "Is your mommy there?"

Instead, she said, "The portrait of Enoch Hayes is finished. I was hoping to talk to Louise to see if she wanted me to bring it over. I have some free time this afternoon."

He was just as businesslike as she was. "That's wonderful news. She was talking about it earlier. She's not here right now—she drove into the village to do some shopping. But she'll be back by one."

"I'll be there at one-thirty then, if you think that's all right. Thank you very much." She hung up the phone and exhaled heavily, stirring the tendrils of bangs across her forehead and slightly fogging her glasses. She had handled that pretty well, all things considered.

"Jenny?" Bennet said to the empty phone line, then held the receiver away from him and studied it glumly for a minute. Well. There was no chance for an apology this time, and it was obvious that she still didn't like him much.

And he probably wouldn't see her this afternoon, as he had arranged a meeting with three of his technical assistants at a country inn on the way to Boston. But Mother would be pleased, anyway. He put the phone down with a feeling of resignation and almost wished he didn't have that meeting.

"Oh, he is just absolutely wonderful! Even the frame is just like the original." Louise looked from the miniature portrait to Jenny, her eyes glowing. "Your friend is so talented. And to answer your question, I'm not at all sure about a portrait of Mrs. Enoch. Let's see. If I remember my family history right, her name was Susannah." Louise looked thoughtfully at the tiny painting in her hand.

"Those portraits were often done in pairs. I just thought there might be one of her," Jenny said.

"The more I think about it, the stranger it seems. You are right, of course. And there is something teasing at the back of my mind—a story I heard when I was a child, I think, though I paid little attention. Children often don't pay attention to what their parents say, even when they are adults. Have you noticed that fact?"

There seemed to be a secondary meaning in the simple statement, but Jenny didn't want to examine it too closely. "And vice-versa, of course," she murmured.

Louise looked slightly puzzled for a moment and then laughed her silvery laugh. "Of course," she agreed. Then, "Can you stay for tea? Mrs. Huckaby makes the most wonderful scones."

Jenny was tempted. Still, she had avoided meeting Bennet this trip so far, and she probably should scoot out of here before he returned. No sense in complicating an otherwise pleasant afternoon, after all.

"Sorry. I left Dad alone, and we have work to do. Perhaps some other time."

"Ah, yes. Bennet told me about your father and the tragic accident. I am so sorry. I hope he is doing all right."

"Thank you. He's reasonably all right, anyway. He's looking forward to working on Birney House."

Louise beamed. "I have so many plans for it. I wish I could get Bennet interested in the project; I think he would be good at it, actually. Oh, speaking of Bennet." She turned to a small table at the side of the blue damask Victorian sofa and picked up a pile of mail. "The postman delivered all of this here instead of to the gatehouse. I wonder, would it be too much trouble for you to drop it off?"

Jenny took a deep breath. "No trouble at all. Shall I just leave it at the door? Is there a box?"

"There is a letter slot in the door. But the French doors that lead from the living room onto the terrace on the right side of the house are usually unlocked. You could leave the letters inside. Bennet usually stacks all his incoming mail on the coffee table in the living room."

"I'll put it on the coffee table, then," Jenny said, staring down at the formidable accumulation of mail. "Goodness. He seems popular."

"Well, yes, he is." There was a quiet maternal pride in Louise's voice, and her chin was tilted upward as she walked Jenny to the front door. "Very popular, I'm glad to say. He gets a great deal of fan mail."

Jenny blinked and tucked that fact away in the back of her mind. "I'll see that he gets it, and let me know if you find any trace of Mrs. Enoch."

"I shall. And come back soon. Bring your father with you, if you'd like. Or perhaps, if it's not too much trouble, may I stop by your place sometime to see your current projects?"

Jenny assured Louise that she was welcome any time, which was certainly true. It might do Dad some good to see a new face. She was sure he'd like Louise.

Less than five minutes later she jiggled the handle of the French doors at the side of the gatehouse. As

Louise had said, the place was not locked. They were trusting people, Jenny thought.

She sidled in, and stopped cold in her tracks, aghast. Such a mess! Books towered and tumbled from every available surface. Papers overflowed the tables, peeked out from under chairs, and erupted up and over the side of the one jam-packed wastebasket.

Notebooks, pens, and pencils were littered everywhere. A bath towel had been tossed over the back of a chair. There was a pair of dirty socks, right under the coffee table, and a sweater dangling precariously at the end of the mantel.

What on earth was all that stuff crowded on the mantel shelf? She took a step closer. It was a collection of frames, plaques, and statuettes, which jostled each other in the limited space.

Awards? She managed to clear a space on the unbelievably cluttered coffee table so that she could deposit her handful of mail, then picked her way through the debris-strewn floor, her gaze fixed unbelieving on the careless array of, yes, awards.

She pushed her glasses up on her nose and leaned forward, peering at the lettering on one of the plaques. Surely one received awards of this type only for legitimate films. What was this? Oh, dear.

Bennet Young, the unbelievable slob, was actually Bennet Young, the maker of impeccable documentaries. No wonder his name had sounded vaguely familiar to her.

"Oh," she said out loud. "Oh, my goodness. Bennet Young. *That* Bennet Young. Of course."

''Of course,'' a deep, smooth voice said from behind her, making her jump with surprise. She smothered a small shriek and clenched her fists. How dare he sneak up on her that way? Indignation fought with guilt, and indignation won. She turned and glared at him. ''Is there another?'' Bennet asked, sounding amused. ''Sorry if I startled you.''

''Why didn't you tell me who you were?''

''You didn't actually ask, did you? Besides, you knew my name, and I told you I was in films. I'm surprised you didn't figure it out. May I ask what you're doing in my living room, anyway?''

Was there a touch of injured pride in his voice? The man certainly had an ego, but perhaps, just perhaps, he was entitled to it. She tried with partial success to fight back the indignation. ''I brought your mail down from the big house,'' she said. ''That pile there, the third from the left on the coffee table.''

''Well. Thank you. Sometime this week, I have to organize all that.''

She looked around her at the chaos. ''That might be a good idea. How do you ever find anything, anyway?''

He didn't miss the note of disapproval in her voice. ''It's actually a very organized mess,'' he told her cheerfully. ''That's the way I work. And it seems to pay off, doesn't it?''

She glanced over at the array of awards and nodded mutely, unable to quibble with obvious success. ''I've enjoyed your work,'' she admitted at last. ''What are you going to do next?''

''Make a pot of coffee,'' he said promptly. ''How

do you like yours?'' He was already heading for a door that led to the kitchen, and she trailed along behind him in spite of herself.

''I can't. Dad will be wondering what happened to me.''

''You can call him if you wish. There's a phone on that table in the hall. Under my jacket, I think. Besides, I want to talk to you about what I'm going to do next besides make coffee. Please stay.''

He said it so nicely, how could she resist? And the phone was, indeed, under his jacket, and coffee sounded good. But she had already told his mother that she couldn't stay for tea, and an edge of guilt niggled at her overly developed conscience along with curiosity about why he wanted to discuss his next project with her.

''Well,'' she said at last, ''I suppose. But just for a little while.''

An hour later she had a pretty good idea of what his next project was going to be.

''Gardens,'' he told her. ''A history of gardens, from the Garden of Eden right on down to today. The Hanging Gardens of Babylon, medieval knot gardens and herb gardens and Kew and Versailles.''

''Mazes,'' Jenny contributed. ''I've always loved mazes.''

''Traditional English gardens and Japanese gardens . . .''

Jenny's mind was racing. ''But why did you want to talk this over with me of all people? I don't know much about gardens.''

"You were singing 'The Sleeping Garden.' Did you know you have a wonderful voice?"

"It's just an ordinary voice," she said, but she was pleased. "I still don't understand." She put her coffee cup down on the space he had cleared at his kitchen table and stared at him.

"All right. An ordinary voice," he acknowledged. She didn't know whether this modification of his previous statement pleased her or not. Mostly not, she decided. He didn't have to agree with her so readily. "But a wonderfully ordinary voice. I don't want to feature any pop, rock, or even opera stars in the film."

She looked at him suspiciously. What was he getting at?

"I heard 'The Sleeping Garden' several years ago at a folk festival in Wales, as a matter of fact, when we were on a shoot. It haunted me. There's a spot in this new film where I want a voice that's natural and attractive and full of haunting color. Like a garden. Like your voice."

There was a warm glow spreading rather traitorously through Jenny's midsection. She was flattered. Yet there was more than flattery in his voice; there was admiration and the edge of something else, something deeper, something that she didn't think she wanted to deal with. . . .

She stared back down into her cup and tried to steel herself. "Oh, I really don't think so, but thank you very much," she said formally, but even she could hear the tiny wistful edge in her voice.

Chapter Five

There was a silence of about five short seconds, which seemed a millennium to Bennet. Why had he asked her, anyway? Probably because, in spite of himself, he found her so attractive. And also because he truly felt her voice would be perfect for the film.

But a tiny voice of reason was telling him, very clearly, that he didn't want to become any closer to Jennifer Blakemore than he absolutely had to. They didn't have the room or the time in their busy lives for each other. He had tried letting a woman into his life once before, and it hadn't been a good idea—then or now.

"Well, think about it, at least," he heard himself saying, deliberately ignoring that carping voice. "I'm still working on scripting and recruiting my crew. You don't have to say yes right at this moment."

It seemed to Jenny that she already had said no right at this moment, but she didn't want to argue the point. "I imagine it must be a lot of hard work, getting something like this started," she said.

He laughed, and he seemed as relieved as she was

to change the subject. "Have you ever really looked at the list of credits at the end of a good documentary?" he asked. "Or don't you watch documentaries?"

"Of course I do!" she flared defensively. Did he think she was a nothing but a soap opera addict? She was, at times, but that was beside the point. Then she added, "Some of them, anyway."

In her mind's eye she could see the endless reel of names. A veritable army of editors, sound people, camera people, consultants, booms and grips and computer specialists and designers and music arrangers and singers . . .

"With all you have to do, I'm sure you're very busy," she said briskly, pushing her chair back from the table. "And I should be getting back to work and to my father too. Thank you for the coffee."

Secretly, she was gratified that he looked surprised at her brusqueness. He was probably used to having people running at his beck and call, she thought. *And I'm not going to sing for him. I'm not.* Though it might be kind of fun. . . .

He was walking very closely beside her as she made her way around the pile of magazines that partially blocked the kitchen door. "I thought maybe we could use a lute or Celtic harp for background," he murmured as if he were tuned in to her thoughts.

Jenny looked up, about to tell him that she was not going to change her mind about singing in his new film. Unfortunately, she wasn't watching where she was going very closely, which was a mistake in Bennet's house. Midway across the living room, her feet became entangled in a haphazard coil of wire that had no business being there and she was thrown right into the protective curve of a strong right arm.

It somehow didn't come as any surprise when the left arm curved around her too, and she found her cheek pressed against a fleecy sweater, her glasses and sense of reality totally askew. Surprisingly she had no impulse whatsoever to pull away, to say a few indignant words about dangerous clutter, to turn her back on Bennet and walk purposefully out of this house.

''You all right?'' Bennet's voice asked against the top of her head, and she tried to nod.

He backed off a couple of inches and looked down at her, then shook his head slightly and lifted the crooked glasses from the bridge of her nose with a smile that blurred as she lost her windows on the world.

''Why such huge specs, anyway?'' he asked, and she could hear the touch of amusement in his voice.

''Because I like . . . to be able . . . to see . . . what I'm doing,'' she answered, breathless and defensive.

''That isn't always necessary, is it?''

His lips were just brushing hers on the last words, and there was no need and no time to answer. The pressure of his kiss increased, but gently, and she felt herself responding to his gentleness though she knew she shouldn't, savoring the warmth and strength of his arms.

It took a surge of inner strength to put both hands on his chest and push herself away. ''Whoa,'' she said, trying to make her voice neutral. ''You made your point. May I have my glasses back?'' The neutral voice wavered embarrassingly.

''For this time.'' He sounded reluctant.

Glasses retrieved, Jenny was relieved that Bennet came back into focus. She glanced up at him quickly. She took illogical comfort in the fact that he looked as surprised as she felt.

And then he said, ''I suppose that I should apologize. But the truth of the matter is, I enjoyed that very much, and there is nothing to apologize for.'' There was a touch of mischief and more than an echo of his mother's speech in the words, and Jenny couldn't restrain a chortle.

The spell was broken, although the words ''for this time'' swirled hauntingly at the back of her mind. She just wouldn't think about them. Not now, at least.

''I understand. It was just a bit of canoodling in the old family tradition,'' she told him kindly, then her voice turned sharp and challenging as she remembered how uncomfortable he had made her feel that day at Birney House. ''You lied about that, didn't you? Why?''

''Lied about . . . oh, Enoch Hayes.'' He shrugged, not looking guilty. ''It was just an impulse. I don't know why. Maybe just to see how you would react.''

''Mmmm.'' He hadn't given her much of an answer. She turned and started again toward the front door, this time warily watching where she was going. ''Speaking of Enoch Hayes, do you happen to remember anything about a portrait of Mrs. Hayes? Your mother wasn't sure, but she thought there might be one tucked away somewhere."

He looked thoughtful. "No. But there are a lot of nooks and crannies up at Birney House where one could be hidden, I suppose. And the attics of Mother's big house are crammed with the flotsam of generations."

Nooks and crannies where the ghosts of yesterdays lurked, attics crammed with wonderful, mysterious trunks and boxes—it was a vision that sounded to Jenny like the next thing to heaven, and she could imagine it all in miniature.

"You and I could look for Mrs. Enoch some time," Bennet was saying, "when you have time. But why do you want her?"

"Susannah," Jenny said absently, now imagining exploring all that with Bennet and trying to squelch a small flutter of entirely uncalled-for excitement. "Her name was Susannah."

"How on earth do you know that?"

"Your mother told me. She'd like to have matching miniature portraits of them, if one of Susannah exists. And it would be nice, wouldn't it, to hang Susannah alongside Enoch after all these years?"

He laughed, and she realized how her words had sounded and laughed with him. "Well, you know what I mean," she added.

They had reached the front door by then, walking close together, as companionable as if they had known each other forever. And yet there was more than companionship in the air, and Jenny knew that she had to put some distance between them, to give herself a chance to think, to be practical.

It was a relief to see the fading green of the fields outside covered with ordinary autumn sunlight, stubbly rough ground stretching away to the blaze of color in the woods across the road. It was a cheerful landscape of uncomplicated reality, one that she could escape into. Time to get back to reality. Time to get back to Dad.

The big dog she had seen with Bennet loped across the top of the porch stairs and lifted his head to bark a greeting at them.

"Move it, Caesar," Bennet growled at the dog. "Miss Blakemore has a tendency to trip over things."

"Now, that's unfair," Jenny started, and felt a flush warming her cheekbones. She stared at the shaggy dog, who had risen to his feet and was staring back at her, darned near eye to eye. "My gosh, he's big!"

"Part sheep dog, part elephant," Bennet said. "He's Mother's dog, actually. I bought him for her a couple of years ago—I didn't much like the idea of Mother and Mrs. Huckaby being out here alone." The dog smiled at him. "But Caesar seems to like it better when I'm home and he can stay with me."

Caesar ambled off and collapsed on the far side of the porch, apparently accepting Jenny as an unthreatening type of human. "I don't suppose you'd have to worry much about trespassers with him around," she said.

"I hope not. He's a cream puff, actually. I'd like it better if Mother would move into town, or at least into a smaller house, like the gatehouse or Birney House. Or even if she'd hire a full-time handyman. She's got room for one. That darned place is too big for just Mother and Mrs. Huckaby. Though Mrs. Huckaby is a gem."

"Too bad *you* don't have a Mrs. Huckaby," Jenny said pointedly, thinking of the unbelievable clutter she had literally stumbled through.

"I don't need another woman running my life," he answered, and though he was smiling, she could sense the seriousness behind his words.

No, of course he didn't. Get real, Jenny. The man is a born loner. "I have to get going," she said quickly. "Dad will wonder what's happened to me."

"And I promised Mother I'd come up and start checking out the electrical system. But it's been fun." He was leaning against a porch post, smiling lazily at her. There was just a hint of mockery in his eyes, a teasing look—a very attractive look. . . .

"I'll see you again, then," she said rather formally, deciding it was best to ignore those last words.

Caesar's good-bye was an enormous friendly bark, more like a roar, as Jenny pulled away from the gatehouse.

Bennet watched her go, frowning. He found her much too appealing. And he would soon be on the road again, traveling through continents with no room in his thoughts for a redheaded imp with huge glasses and a sweet voice.

But he already knew it was too late to think that way. She had drifted into his thoughts, snuggling into a warm corner of his heart, no matter where on earth he happened to be. Just what was he supposed to do about that?

He ran his hands impatiently through his thick mane of hair and, unexpectedly, wondered if his hairline would recede over the coming years the way his father's had. A brief, vivid mental snapshot of himself flashed through his mind, twenty years older, thinning hair, still alone, still seeing the world as if it were part of some vast documentary. That was the great thing. He had his work—his totally absorbing work.

And right now he also had Mother's electrical system to take a look at. He whistled to Caesar, who lumbered to his feet with incredible lightness considering his size and looked hopefully at Bennet.

"Come on, we'll walk up to the house," he told the dog. "You need the exercise and so do I."

"I am so glad you are here, dear, but do leave that monster outside. He makes the Meissen figures tremble in their case when he walks across the floor."

"He'll wait on the porch," Bennet told his mother. "But you really shouldn't call him a monster, you know. You'll hurt his feelings."

She sniffed. "I don't believe he has any feelings—just an enormous appetite. I am fond of him, of course, but if I wanted a horse I would have bought one. I much prefer miniatures."

"A yapping little poodle isn't much of a watchdog, Mother."

"I was not necessarily referring to miniature *dogs,* Bennet."

He felt it would be safer to change the subject. "I'll start with the fuse box," he told her. "You say that it's the lights in the library that are the worst? Let's see what I can find."

An hour later Mrs. Huckaby brought fresh coffee and creamy lemon bars to the kitchen table and retreated to rehang newly laundered lace curtains in the south bedroom.

"She has too much to do," Bennet said accusingly. "Can't you get someone in to help her?"

Louise sighed. "We had two or three girls from town. They didn't work out. There was an older woman who tried to tell Mrs. Huckaby how to run things too."

"I can see that wouldn't work," he said dryly. "Keep trying. Or else move to a smaller place."

"This house is full of memories, Bennet. I hate to leave."

"It's also full of questionable wiring," Bennet told her. "I think you should have an electrician come in. I did some splicing and replaced some sockets but both the plumbing and wiring in this place are due for an overhaul."

"I just dislike all the mess involved, Bennet, but I will make arrangements if you think it necessary. Now. You did get your mail this afternoon?" She was smiling slightly, looking surprisingly youthful and conspiratorial in her matching gray-blue sweater and slacks. She watched with eyes that missed little.

"You sent the mailperson yourself, I take it?"

"It seemed convenient. My feelings should be hurt, though. She turned me down for tea, but stayed at the gatehouse for a while, did she not?"

"Mother, do you have the binoculars out again?" Bennet asked with a touch of exasperation. "Yes, she stayed for a short time at my request." The corner of his mouth twitched upward. "I think she finds my normal working clutter a little overwhelming."

"No doubt." She was still watching him with that see-all look that had always made him uncomfortable. "And I believe you find her attractive, am I right? How nice. How very nice."

"You look as if you had a good afternoon." George scanned his daughter's face, noting the extra sparkle in the expressive eyes behind the oversize glasses. He tried to smile at her, but a sharp twinge of pain across his temples drowned the smile before it was fully formed.

"It was all right—Dad, what's wrong?"

"Nothing much. The usual little devils with pitchforks jabbing at me when I don't expect it." He wheeled his chair away from her, hoping to escape her probing gaze. "You stayed for a while."

A tingle of guilt caught at Jenny's heart. "Oh, Dad, I'm sorry. I didn't mean to stay so long. You must be starved to death. It's already nearly six." He looked gray and drawn, even more so than usual. She shouldn't have left him for so long, she thought.

"No, I'm not that hungry." That was true enough. "Liz brought over sandwiches and played gin with me for a while. I guess I'm just tired. I really didn't mean that you had been gone for too long.'' It was his turn for guilty pangs; Jenny had a right to a life of her own and rarely got a chance to just be herself.

''I'll fix that chicken and rice casserole you like. It won't take long in the microwave.''

He could hear the concern in her voice. He continued to be such a burden to this child. For she was still a child to him: barely out of carrot-colored pigtails, all long legs and lopsided smile. ''That would be nice,'' he said, not looking at her. Then he added, ''Jenny, I'd like to go back to Boston for an evaluation. Maybe they could find something that would help speed up this whole blasted process.''

''I've been thinking the same thing,'' Jenny told him softly. ''But I was afraid you wouldn't want to go. The last time I mentioned it you got so angry.''

''I want to. I want to get better. I want—I don't know what I want.''

''Right now you probably want a cup of tea and a fire in the fireplace. And the evening news.''

''I'm not a helpless invalid, Jenny,'' he said with an edge to his voice. ''I'll fix a salad.'' But he didn't feel like doing any such thing. Once again the thought that both of them would have been better off if he had died in the accident stabbed painfully across his consciousness, and once more he tried to push all the negativity away. It was getting harder to do.

Dinner was a quiet affair. Jenny was lost in her thoughts, which was just as well, as he didn't feel like talking much. He ate a small portion just to please her, but he was happy to settle in front of the television after the dishes were done and doze and fight the slight feeling of illness that never seemed to leave.

Jenny went out to the workshop. She was carefully ''aging'' the tiny brick courtyard outside the side door to Gillyflower Cottage, ''planting'' minute daisies and delphinium for an English country garden look. She wished Dad felt up to helping. Maybe tomorrow. . . .

Jenny worked quietly, not singing as she so often did. Her mind kept straying annoyingly from what she was doing, straying to the afternoon with Bennet, to the kiss she had enjoyed so much. There. She had admitted it. Her hand jerked almost imperceptibly and pulled a tendril of ivy away from the side of the house. Darn.

Gardens, was it? It sounded like such a wonderful project. She looked down at her tiny courtyard—her re-creation of an English garden—and sighed at the row of clay pots she had just carelessly knocked across the bricks. No harm done, but her mind definitely wasn't where it should be.

Around eight the ringing of the phone startled them both. Jenny caught it, hurrying in from the workshop with a daub of pink paint smeared across one cheekbone.

''Jenny, this is Liz. Is your dad all right? I just thought I'd check, because he looked pretty peaked this afternoon.''

''He's okay.''

''You don't sound like you mean that.''

''Well, I don't think it's one of his best days. But

he's decided he wants to go back to Boston for a complete evaluation. It's probably a good idea. They might be able to help."

There was a brief silence at the other end of the line. Then, "That sounds like a wonderful idea, Jenny." Liz's voice was warm and compassionate. "We'll get him walking yet. And in the meantime, he can help you finish up Gillyflower. It's such a wonderful house."

"Thanks, Liz, for everything. For bringing over sandwiches too. I don't know what I'd do without you."

"I enjoy every minute I spend with your dad, Jenny. Don't ever hesitate to call when you need me."

I couldn't ask for a better neighbor, Jenny thought as she put the phone down. She glanced into the living room. Dad was apparently asleep. Sadness, hope, and a dull, unidentified longing slipped through the back corridors of Jenny's mind. She was tired. It was time to call it a day.

Getting Dad into bed took longer than usual that night, and Jenny almost fell asleep in a cloud of jasmine-scented bubbles in the tub. She jerked herself back to full consciousness reluctantly.

She had been wandering through an exotic eastern garden where bowers of jasmine and roses and sandalwood bloomed, and a tall, dark-haired man had walked beside her, his arm around her.

Dreamer, she told herself sarcastically, fully awake. *Darned fool dreamer.*

* * *

For three or four days she made a point of staying close to Dad, to watch and assess while she worked on the finishing touches to Gillyflower Cottage. He was making an effort to help, to be cheerful. With his blessing, she called the specialist in Boston who had worked with him right after the accident.

Yes, the doctor agreed, it was time for a reevaluation. He sounded puzzled, and asked Jenny if she thought part of the problem was psychological. Jenny guardedly—and reluctantly—admitted that possibility. The doctor said he would contact a colleague of his, an excellent psychiatrist who dealt with trauma recovery, and they set up a tentative appointment for two weeks hence. Jenny thanked him and crossed her fingers. Maybe there was a faint candle glow at the end of the tunnel.

Louise called her the next Monday. "Somewhere at Birney House, probably in the attic, there is a pine table that's supposed to be a genuine Shaker piece. It was used in the kitchen years ago. I would very much like to have a copy of it. I thought perhaps your father. . . ."

"Shaker pieces are relatively easy," Jenny told her. "I'm sure Dad would be happy to do it."

"And I believe there is also a spinning wheel there. As well as a spinning Jenny. I was thinking about you yesterday, Jenny, when I remembered both of them. An obvious connection, as you can see."

Jenny chuckled. "Obviously. Do you have photos and measurements?"

"Well, no, dear. I thought perhaps you would rather

do that yourself, to make sure everything was perfectly exact. But perhaps you would have tea with me on Wednesday? And bring your father, if you think he would enjoy seeing the house."

"That's very nice of you. I'll see how he feels on Wednesday. It would probably do both of us good to get away for a few hours."

Almost predictably, her father shook his head when Wednesday arrived. "Not this time, Jen. I'm not quite up to it. But maybe the next time? After we've seen the doctor? I'll stay here and work on those mullioned windows that are sticking."

"Well, okay. But be sure to call Liz if you need anything."

"Like a game of Scrabble if my fingers start to knot up on me. My hands don't always work the way they used to, I'm afraid."

She kissed him on the top of the head. "You'll do just fine. I'll be back in time to fix dinner. Stay out of trouble while I'm gone."

He smiled at her, a glint of his old sense of humor lighting his eyes. "If Bennet is there, *you* stay out of trouble, young lady."

She made a disparaging noise and left, but his words needled at her as she headed the van toward the Youngs'. Was she that transparent? Did the fact that Bennet was on her mind a lot show in her traitorous, open-book face?

She never could put anything over on Dad. Besides, Bennet might not be at his mother's house this afternoon. She hoped he wouldn't be—or did she hope he *would* be?

Sighing, she swung past the gatehouse. There was no sign of Bennet's van. He was probably away. Very Important Film People who put out documentaries had to be on the go a lot, after all.

Mrs. Huckaby answered the door, her manner a little warmer than the first time Jenny had visited the house. Right behind her was Bennet. Jenny caught her breath. He looked darkly handsome, in a gray sweater and black turtleneck. Why did he have to be here, anyway? Why did he have to make her heart thump the way it did? Why did he have to look so darned irresistible?

"Why don't you give me your jacket?" Bennet said. "I'll put it in the guest closet. And you can leave your bag and camera down here on the hall table. We'll go up to Birney House a little later. Mother has been waiting for you. I could hardly keep her from running down the stairs to greet you."

"Thank you," Jenny said automatically, handing him her dark blue plaid blazer and smoothing her navy sweater over her hips. Wait, what he had just said? "She's upstairs?" she tried. Why couldn't Louise come to greet her?

"I'm afraid she took a bad fall yesterday," Bennet said grimly, "up at Birney House. Those stairs can be treacherous."

"Oh, good heavens. Why didn't you let me know? We could have postponed this."

"You still don't know Mother very well, do you? She would have to be in intensive care before she'd tell you not to come. Nothing broken, thank goodness, but her back is sprained and she has to rest for a few days.''

Poor Louise. So it looked as if Jenny would be looking at that table at Birney House with Bennet, after all. That was great. Just great. And she realized as those words formed in her mind that she wasn't being entirely sarcastic.

Careful, she told herself sternly. She followed him up the broad staircase, acutely aware of the controlled energy of his movements. If she hadn't been here, she was sure he would have taken the steps two at a time. And she bet that when he was small, he had slid down that graceful curved banister more than once. *She* certainly would have.

Just inside Louise's doorway, she stopped and caught her breath, all thoughts of banister-sliding chased from her mind.

The room imprinted itself on her mind like a sharp-edged photograph. It was furnished with a richly carved Victorian Belter bedstead covered with lacy blue and white linens, matching Belter chairs, carved armoire, and what looked to be Tiffany lamps on the bedside stands. The walls and draperies were silvery blue trimmed with white. The same subtle tones were repeated in the background of the carpet, with its pastel floral overlay.

''Oh, I wish I could put it in a box,'' she murmured aloud before she could stop herself.

''You wish you could do *what?*'' Bennet's surprised

voice asked from close beside her, and there was a soft chuckle from the direction of the bed.

She caught herself. Where were her manners? She smiled at the tiny woman sitting propped on billowy pillows in the exact center of the picture-perfect bed.

"Forgive me, Louise. It's an occupational disease. I meant that your room would make an absolutely beautiful miniature room box."

"Thank you. Yes, that sounds like a wonderful project. I might be tempted to start on it right away if people around here would just let me out of bed."

"No way," Bennet told her firmly.

"I'm sorry you got hurt," Jenny said with sympathy. "But it's something you could think about."

"I am quite tired of thinking, reading, and working crossword puzzles, thank you," the older woman grumbled gently. "Though I am very fortunate that it wasn't worse. Have you ever watched soap operas? I believe I could become addicted."

The small TV on a stand near the bed was off now, but Jenny smiled. "Dad did, for a while," she said.

There was a brief, awkward silence, and then Louise said, "I am so sorry, Jenny. I will be back on my feet soon, and I have no cause to complain. How is your father doing?"

"He could be better." She made a determined effort to smile. "We're working on it."

"I am looking forward to meeting him some day—before too long, I hope. Now, Bennet, shall I ring for Mrs. Huckaby to bring us tea and cookies, or will you go and get them and give her a rest?"

It was obvious what Louise wanted him to do, and he moved toward the door. "I'll go. She's been running around enough in the last few days. I'll give her a rest now that I'm back."

"Thank you, dear." Louise watched her son leave the room with a particularly thoughtful look. "It was those back stairs at Birney House," she said suddenly when he was out of sight. "They are so steep. You may have noticed."

"Yes, I did." There was something on Louise's mind. Jenny waited.

"Extremely steep, and I did slip, actually, only a few steps. But I could not get up right away. I kept thinking that if I could just make it to my car, I could get home." She glanced up at Jenny. "I was alone, you know. I hadn't even taken Caesar with me. He doesn't fit in my car anyway." She hesitated for a heartbeat. "At any rate, I did think I was alone. Still—"

"Still?" Jenny prompted, almost holding her breath. There was a strange note in Louise's voice.

"It could have been my imagination, of course. But I thought I heard something moving quietly in the kitchen, and a door closing. I suppose it was a draft, or something of that sort. I don't want to mention it to Bennet. He would think I imagined it. But I don't think it was my imagination. And it was a little bit frightening."

Chapter Six

"More than a little bit, I should think." Jenny bit her bottom lip, watching Louise closely. Yes, it could have been a draft, but whatever it was, Jenny didn't think Louise had imagined it. "I do think you should tell Bennet about it so he can check it out."

"Yes, my dear, I expect you are right." She gazed at Jenny for a moment and then dropped her eyes, her fingers playing with the lacy edge of the sheet. "But I was hoping that when the two of you go up to Birney House this afternoon, you could keep an eye out for anything that looks unusual, perhaps?"

"Of course. But two sets of eyes are better than one. And Bennet is more familiar with the house."

Louise sighed resignedly. "Again, you are right. It is just that, well, Bennet worries about me. If he thinks I am imagining things, he will worry about my mental health. If he thinks there has been an intruder at Birney House, he will worry about my safety. And he has to be away so much. You do understand, don't you?"

I do indeed, Jenny thought, both concerned and amused. "How about if I just play it by ear when we get there, Louise? It may help to explain why I'm poking into odd nooks and crannies.''

Louise laughed. ''Go right ahead, if you feel it necessary. Although you could always say you were looking for the portrait of Susannah Hayes, I suppose.''

''Or any stray resident ghost. He'd probably believe that too.''

''Are you talking about me?'' Bennet's deep voice came from the doorway. ''What is it I'd be so gullible about?''

''That I might be looking for ghosts at Birney House,'' Jenny answered quickly. ''To reproduce in miniature.''

''Well,'' he said, setting the tray he was carrying on a small table near Louise's bed, ''at least that would be interesting, and probably right in character. I'll be glad to help. Now, do you take sugar and lemon with your tea?''

He was making such a wonderful effort to be pleasant and impersonal. Jenny wondered if he even remembered that he had kissed her, or whether it was just such a casual thing to him that he had completely put it out of his mind.

She sneaked a quick sideways look at him. He was watching her over the top of his teacup with a look that hinted very strongly that he wasn't at all the forgetful type. She looked away again with a pleasant shiver.

They drove to Birney House in his van. Huge clouds had gathered at the edges of an improbably blue sky, and a fitful wind sent a bright confetti of leaves skittering wildly across the gravel road. Birch leaves like golden coins were scattered across the shrubs that surrounded the old house, and to Jenny it was more of a perfect picture than the first time she had seen it.

Inside, the sun slanting through the wavy panes of old glass showed the slight film of dust over everything. If anyone had been here, Jenny thought, it would be obvious. There would be a disarrangement of the sense of time that lay so lightly on the house, of the dust.

Caesar had begged to come with them, and now padded closely in their footsteps when they entered the house. Jenny glanced down at him. He would know too, if there was a stranger in the house, wouldn't he? Or even someone not so strange, but a shadow from the past who still lingered? He looked back at her with mild curiosity. He apparently didn't sense anything sinister about the house, but she couldn't quite still the little fingers of apprehension that fluttered down her spine, a feeling that just might have something to do with the man who walked beside her.

"I think the table is up in the attic," Bennet said as they passed through the kitchen. Then, as they started up the narrow staircase that turned abruptly upward at the corner of the kitchen, he said, "This is where Mother fell. If she'd actually broken her hip, or her ankle, it might have been hours before Mrs. Huckaby came to look for her."

"I know. I'm glad nothing like that happened." She stood still for a moment at the bottom of the stairs, looking back at the cavernous kitchen as if she might see some sign of whatever or whoever had been there. But of course there was nothing. And maybe there hadn't been anything that other day, either.

"You go first. I'll come behind you in case you should slip."

Obeying, she looked back over her shoulder at him with the hint of a smile. "Don't worry," she said. "I'm only too aware of the dangers."

"Are you, now?" He didn't think that she was. He didn't think that she was aware at all of the emotions she stirred in him, protective and otherwise.

He was the one who would have to be careful, very careful. No woman—and especially a woman like this one, with all her responsibilities—would fit into his life. But oh, how well she fit into his arms.

Caesar padded behind them as far as the second floor, and then, with a whuffle and a moan, collapsed on the floor with his head on his mammoth paws and his eyes rolled up slightly. If these humans, he seemed to say, wanted to climb that last narrow, impossible stairway, which led up to who knew what, let them go. He was smarter than that.

Bennet chuckled at the dog and pulled the chain that brought a low watt bulb to life. It didn't help much, but at least they weren't entirely enveloped in darkness. "Watch it," he said to Jenny.

"Right," she answered in a low voice. She stopped suddenly, looking up into the narrow passageway, and he nearly collided with her. He caught the faint floral scent of shampoo in her hair and closed his eyes, clenching his hands to keep from reaching out and smoothing that wavy coppery mass that was caught against its will at the back of her neck.

Then they were at the top of the stairs and could move a little farther apart, and he began to feel sanity return, though reluctantly. Again, he pulled a chain to bring an inadequate bulb to life.

"It's dark up here, but oh, just look," she said in awe.

He looked. To him, it appeared to be nothing more than the Birney House dump: forgotten boxes, battered furniture, stacks of books—everything covered with a generous coat of dust and festooned with cobwebs. Something about it reminded him of his living room at the cottage.

"We should have brought a flashlight, I guess. Those little windows aren't much use," he said.

She pushed her glasses up on her nose and moved a few steps away from him, looking around avidly. "Your eyes get used to the gloom. It's wonderful."

"Wonderful," he muttered. "Sure."

"Oh, come on, Bennet. Don't you feel the sense of continuity, the family history all around you? Where's your imagination?"

"Guess I'll have to try looking through your eyes. Maybe it's your glasses that do it."

She turned to give him a look that was half exasperated, half amused. "Use your imagination, Bennet," she reminded him. "You must have one, to do the work you do."

"Certainly I have one," he said, stung. He studied the outline of her form against the light from the tiny, grimy window at the south end of the attic. He wanted to reach out and touch her, make sure she was real.

A small frown tugged at her eyebrows as she studied him. ‘‘An attic can be a very special place,’’ she said at last. ‘‘So much to look at.’’

‘‘And do you like what you see?’’ There was laughter in his voice.

She turned away from him quickly, sure he was teasing, playing games with her. ‘‘Very much,’’ she said, trying to keep her voice light. ‘‘Look. In the corner. There's the wheel and the jenny.’’

Relieved to break away from the layers of attraction that shimmered between them like the dust itself, she picked her way carefully across the floor. Camera ready, she took several shots, hoping her hand was steady.

‘‘The table's over here, I think,’’ he offered from behind her. They were normal words, spoken in a normal voice, and she gave a little sigh. It was a sigh of relief, she told herself.

‘‘Oh, good. Yes, it's Shaker all right.’’ She dug her tape measure out of the bottom of her bag and moved toward the table—and toward Bennet. It was hard to keep any distance between them up here. And she knew instinctively that distance was crucial.

‘‘Perfect proportion and construction,’’ she murmured, pulling out the drawer to check the dovetailing. She backed away, camera clicking. Then, out of the corner of her eye she saw the frames stacked against the rough beams halfway across the attic. ‘‘Better check those out. Susannah just might be there.’’

He wasn't sure what she was talking about until he saw she was gently prying apart the tangle of frames. And then he moved to help her sort them out, watching her study each one, so intent, so involved. So appealing.

"Interesting, but no Susannah." She straightened at last, looking slightly disappointed. "Nice landscapes and some great old photos, though. They should be hung someplace where they can be seen." She backed away, not looking where she was going.

It was the old croquet mallet that did it. She stepped on the edge of it and felt her ankle twist underneath her, sending her sideways. Without Bennet's quick reaction and his strong arm, she would have fallen.

She closed her eyes against the pain and managed what she felt was a very restrained "ouch."

"Are you—are you all right?" He spoke into her hair, his breath stirring little whispers of warmth at her ear.

She clung to him for that moment, because it was the only thing she could do. His sweater was warm and soft against her cheek, and his arms felt so protective, and dangerous.

"Maybe if I sit down for just a minute," she tried. "Just pulled something in my ankle, that's all." Backing away from him with reluctance, she looked around. There was a flattop steamer trunk a few feet away that would do. Her knees as well as her ankle felt weak at that moment.

He took a deep breath. "You'll get all dusty," was

all he could manage to say when she lowered herself gratefully onto the trunk.

"Minor detail," she said, rubbing her ankle and thinking about those steep stairs. "It's okay."

He sat down beside her, though there wasn't much room. "Can I do anything?"

"No," she answered quickly, afraid he might want to take over the ankle-rubbing. "It feels better already." Desperately, she searched for something impersonal to say. "How's your project coming?"

"Great," he replied after a moment's pause, still watching her rub her ankle. The cobwebs in this attic must be getting inside his head, because for a few seconds he couldn't imagine what she was talking about. "We got a commitment for some major funding this week."

"So you'll be off filming soon."

"I suppose I will. Are you going to sing for me?"

"Well. Maybe. I'll think about it." She sat up straight and flexed her ankle. It would be all right; she didn't think there was an actual sprain. She glanced at her watch. "I probably should get back to Dad."

He nodded slowly. There it was again, that sense of responsibility. Was there some way he could get across that bridge, care about her, love her, be with her while he could, without any long-term commitment? Probably not.

"Do you think he'll get better, really?"

She shivered slightly. That was a question she didn't want to think too closely about, and yet she had to.

"I don't know any more. I used to think so. But I

don't know whether it's physical or emotional. He feels so much guilt.''

''Because he was driving when the accident happened?''

''Partly. Partly because he feels he's interfered with my life. Partly because he and Mother moved to Wellston years ago, and he would drive to the coast and spend most of the week there to run the business. He feels he didn't spend enough time with her.''

''It's complicated. I'm sorry.'' She had taken her glasses off and was rubbing her eyes. He just couldn't help it. He reached out and pulled her to him, kissing her temple, wanting to take care of things, which was something that he just couldn't do.

Still, with his forefinger, he tilted her chin toward him and let his lips taste hers: softly, gently. It might be madness, but it was such wonderful madness.

There was a sudden flurry of sharp, deep-throated barking from the bottom of the attic stairs.

Bennet lifted his head with reluctance. ''What's he trying to say?'' he asked in a husky voice, not sure whether he was glad or sorry for the interruption.

Jenny sat up straight, settling her glasses back in place, ashamed of her unexpected show of emotion. ''I don't know, I'm sure,'' she said primly, but her voice was slightly uneven. ''I don't speak dog.''

''We'd better check. Maybe there's someone here.''

A tiny chill of intuition chilled its way through Jenny's mind and nerves. She couldn't have explained how she knew, but she was certain: Someone was here, all right. Someone who Louise had also sensed in Birney House.

Someone or something.

Ten minutes later, Jenny still felt that certainty, though they had found no sign of anyone. Her ankle was a little uncomfortable, but not nearly as uncomfortable as that uneasy feeling that they weren't entirely alone. And hadn't she felt something of the sort the first time she had been in Birney House?

Caesar padded along beside them, sniffing in corners and looking at them curiously, seeming to have forgotten that he was the one who had sounded the alarm in the first place.

"Maybe he just got tired of waiting for us," Jenny suggested, even though it hadn't sounded like that kind of bark.

"Hail Caesar, mighty communicator," Bennet told the dog with disgust. "Dumb dog. Come on, we might as well check out the cellar."

Predictably, the cellar stairs were narrow and dark, leading down from a small door just off the kitchen and disappearing into what looked like a black pit. Jenny was glad she wasn't claustrophobic. But when Bennet flipped the light switch at the top of the stairs, at least three bulbs sprang to life, and she gave a sigh of relief.

Hearing the sigh, he hesitated and looked down at her, misinterpreting. "Hey, look, your ankle is probably sore. You've gone up and down enough stairs for now. Why don't you stay up here with Caesar while

I check things out down there?'' The gentle concern in his voice caused a strange lump to rise in her throat.

It was tempting to stay safely with Caesar, but she was curious. And there was much more to it than curiosity, she knew. Those few minutes they had shared in the attic before Caesar disturbed them had been unbearably sweet. If she stayed close to him, maybe she could retain and hoard some of that sweetness, that warmth, tuck it deep in her heart so it wouldn't disappear entirely.

It would be something to take home to savor in her memory during the chill autumn nights. Something to remember at the same time that she sensibly talked herself out of any involvement with this man, because any kind of involvement just wouldn't work. Between his career and her father's needs, there was little chance of future for them. She simply couldn't allow herself to fall in love with him.

The fact that the word ''love'' was in her thoughts surprised her. The logical part of her mind resisted it. *Get hold of yourself, Jennifer Blakemore*. It was nothing but a physical attraction, very easily transcended if she just put her mind to it.

''My ankle's perfectly all right and I do want to see the cellar,'' she told him with determination, unable to look directly into his eyes. She was afraid he would read the attraction in her own. And that just wouldn't be smart.

''Stubborn woman.'' There was a just a hint of laughter in his voice.

''You'd better believe it.''

Caesar had already padded clumsily to the foot of the stairs, looking back up over his shoulder at them with obvious impatience. When they reached the bottom, the dog paced heavily from one side of the cellar to the other, nose down, whuffling from time to time as if he found this very interesting indeed.

Jenny said tentatively, "It doesn't look as if there's been anyone down here, does it? I mean, it has such a quiet, undisturbed feeling to it. What on earth could Caesar be looking for?"

"Mmmm." Bennet was watching Caesar with a slight frown. "It might be that he's sensed a rat, or a racoon, or some small animal. He's certainly not getting excited over it."

There was storage space down here too: room for old cans of paint, a stack of magazines disintegrating into dust, shelves with odds and ends of hardware and old tools stacked on them. A shelving unit held nothing but cans of fruit and vegetables and some empty canning jars. A large, old coal furnace took up one end of the space.

Jenny turned to look around her, her mind automatically measuring as it always did, though she had no particular desire to turn this nondescript cellar into a miniature room. The walls were dark and dingy, and supporting beams rode massively overhead and along the sides of the walls, which could have been concrete or hard-packed earth.

"This wasn't part of the original house, was it?" she asked.

"No. If I remember correctly, many years ago they

enlarged a primitive root cellar and shored up the sides when the furnace was put in.''

''But it doesn't extend the entire length of the house.'' Her mental measurements had told her that much. She shivered slightly at the webs festooning the walls and beams. ''Nothing much down here but a good collection of spid—''

Her words were cut off by three hoarse roars from Caesar. Over by the furnace, the dog stood with head lowered, staring at the shadowy dark behind the base of the furnace. He followed up the roars with a menacing growl, and then seemed to change his mind, wagged his tail, straightened his head, and lumbered back over to sit beside Bennet, looking extraordinarily pleased with himself.

Sometime during this outburst Bennet had taken her hand. She let it stay there, momentarily tempted to lean against him for support. Caesar's deep-throated barks reverberated in the enclosed underground space, and she was more startled than she wanted to admit.

''Why did he . . .'' she started. Then, since Caesar had obviously decided that he was mistaken about whatever it was that he had seen or heard, ''Oh, I *do* wish he wouldn't do things like that. His voice is so—so *huge*.'' She sagged against Bennet in spite of herself, and he released her hand to put his arm protectively around her waist.

He chuckled involuntarily, even as his arm tightened and he pulled her close to his side. ''You know, you sounded exactly like Mother just then,'' he told her.

Oh, boy, he was laughing at her and being protective

at the same time. She hated to be laughed at and she certainly didn't need protecting, but she didn't move away. A peculiar chill of uncertainty lingered in her thoughts, dragging like the skeletal fingers of a ghost across the back of her neck.

"He probably just heard a mouse." Bennet's matter-of-fact tone helped calm her tingling nerve endings. "It's all right." She managed to give him a quick smile and then take a sidways step away from him, though her hand was still firmly clasped in his and she had neither the strength nor the desire to remove it. "Well, all right," he said, looking a little quizzical, even slightly hurt. "Okay, then. I take it you're ready to go back upstairs?"

"Yes," she said in a small voice.

At that moment she saw the door behind the furnace. Squat and wide, its outline was almost invisible in the deep shadows. "What's behind the door?" she asked, glad for something to divert her mind. Maybe it was a storage room. Maybe there were treasures there. Maybe it even held the lost portrait of Susannah Hayes.

"The coal room," Bennet said. "It's pretty small, just big enough to hold a load of coal. There's a chute that leads up to a little window, where the coal truck used to deliver. I played in there when I was a child, and I'd get absolutely filthy and drive Mother nuts. It's been empty for years, since the furnace was put in. Want to take a look, if I can get that sticky bolt loose?"

The massive bolt that secured the door did look as if it had been in place for many years. "No," she decided. "I've seen a coal bin before. Let's go up—it's getting late."

"Right." Bennet released her hand reluctantly and watched her start up the stairs with that unconscious grace of hers, not looking back at him, her back as straight as a ramrod. He shook his head imperceptibly, whistled Caesar back to his side, and followed her.

What was going on between them was strange, sort of like a dance that had to be performed without looking at or touching your partner. They were connecting, somehow, and yet there was so much left unsaid. A rational voice deep inside told him it was probably because they were both afraid of getting too close. Still, it wasn't his fault, was it?

Jenny spent only another twenty minutes or so with Louise, telling her they had found the table and the spinning jenny and wheel and she would set Dad to work on them soon. She also told Louise there didn't appear to be an intruder at Birney House. It had probably been just the old house settling, creaking—a draft, as Louise had suspected. But Jenny herself didn't quite believe that, and wasn't sure why she didn't.

Bennet had excused himself almost as soon as they arrived back at the big house, saying he had a couple of phone calls to make and papers to go through. Both he and Louise urged Jenny to come back soon.

She promised she would. But, she told herself as she drove back toward Wellston, it would definitely be better if she stayed away for a while. She could keep in touch with Louise by phone. By the time she went back to see her personally, once work had begun on the miniature Birney House, maybe Bennet would be off on one of his trips. That certainly would be better.

Still, she couldn't help glancing at the gatehouse as she went by for any sign of Bennet. Caesar was flopped under a tree in the side yard, and Bennet's van was there, but he was nowhere in sight.

He was making calls and doing paperwork. She had a brief vivid vision of the disarray—no, the complete and utter mess—that lay around him as he worked, unless some shining miracle of intensive housecleaning had taken place. She shook the vision away and resolutely thought of other things.

She could hear the low hum of voices from the workroom when she entered the house, then Liz's throaty laugh. At least Dad hadn't been alone all afternoon.

Liz was perched on Jenny's stool, watching Dad at the workbench. He was raking fine model railroad ballast, the rich "loam" for the miniature English garden, into glue that was dotted along the base of Gillyflower's side wall. Trellises and rose bushes and morning glories already added color to the three-inch strip.

He had managed to get quite a bit done today, and he smiled a contented half smile as he sprinkled a little fine moss into the gaps, forming low mounds that could be herbs.

Unexpectedly, Jenny thought of rosemary and remembrance and of the possibility of singing in Bennet's new film. No, she couldn't. She just couldn't do it.

She wrenched her mind away from Bennet. "Well!"

she said too brightly from the doorway. ''What a beautiful job! Are you becoming a miniature gardener, Liz?''

Liz and Dad both turned toward her, Liz's eyes round with surprise. ''Oh, Jenny,'' she said. ''I didn't hear you come in. Me, a miniature gardener?'' She looked down at her ample body with a small laugh. ''I couldn't be a miniature anything. Your dad is so good at it, though.'' Liz looked at George with something, Jenny noted wryly, that approached sheer adoration. ''It takes a special touch, doesn't it?''

''It does, and he has it,'' Jenny agreed, while her father smiled and shrugged.

''Have a good afternoon?'' he asked.

''Very.'' She kept her voice light. It was probably a good thing that he didn't know how confused her heart and mind were. ''From the look of things, it won't be long before we can get a good start on Birney House, will it?''

''The closer it gets to being done, the more beautiful it is,'' Liz said, the beam of her adoring gaze now directed at Gillyflower. ''I just love it. But I've got to get home now too. I was making double chocolate milkshakes an hour ago and had so much that I just thought I'd bring some over to your dad.'' She picked up the two tall glasses and rose, smiling at Jenny. ''I should let you get to work, after all.''

''Thanks, Liz,'' Jenny told her neighbor as they walked together to the front door. ''I appreciate your checking on him.''

''My pleasure.'' Liz beamed. ''Honest.''

And she really means that, Jenny thought to herself, watching Liz make her way through the gap in the fence between their houses. She definitely had designs on her father—not that it would do her a bit of good. Not a bit. Some romances were just never meant to be. She walked thoughtfully back to the workroom to help Dad add the finishing touches to the garden.

That had sure been a close call.

He could breathe again now. They were gone, along with that bigmouthed dog. It had sounded like a man and a woman, although he hadn't risked peeking through the crack in the door. He hadn't dared to even move his little finger once he had scuttled back into the coal room and let the bolt fall back into place.

It was a good thing he had rigged up that little lock with fishing line and a thin piece of aluminum. He could still use his mind and hands well enough when he had to. He had found that out in the last few weeks, and the knowledge had helped.

This little coalhole was a heck of a lot better than a box in a city back alley or a dark doorway. Maybe he had been smart to run, though at the time his mind had been so muddled from drink that he didn't know what he was running to—or running from, for that matter. Running from death, probably, come to think of it.

He turned on the tiny light beside the door. He had remembered enough from his construction days to run wiring in here. So he had a light, a camp stove, and a few other camping supplies he had found in the shed out back. And a reasonably warm, dry place to sleep.

But he couldn't stay here forever. Small tingles of guilt kept nagging at him: He had no real right to stay here, and the people who lived here might come back soon. He had to stand on his own two feet.

At least his hands didn't shake much any more. He stared down at them—broad hands, but aging wrinkles on the palms now where the calluses used to be. Used to be a man's hands, but now they looked old and soft, like him. He ran them through his thinning hair and sighed.

He hadn't had a drink now for almost six weeks. *Maybe there's hope for you yet, Ben Williams,* he told himself, *start living again one of these days.* Without Alice, though, it wouldn't be easy. If the kids hadn't moved away, if Alice hadn't got sick and died, if he had been a stronger man. . . .

No sense in always saying "if." If he had a grain of sense in his head he never would have gotten into this fix. But that was water under the bridge, wasn't it?

Don't start feeling sorry for yourself, he told himself sternly. It was time to fix something to eat, and then he could sneak out for an evening walk through the woods, where the trees fed his soul and the moon and stars lit his way toward peace.

Things could be so much worse.

Chapter Seven

Jenny talked to herself a lot over the next few days. It was an effort to keep that intensely personal conversation with herself completely within her own mind and not ramble on aloud. Dad would think she was losing it completely if he could hear her jumbled thoughts.

It was crazy, it was impossible, it was just not smart. She couldn't be falling for Bennet. Yet the memory of his arms, of his kisses, got hold of her when she wasn't on guard and shook her, both mentally and physically, clear to her toes.

Darn it, she really *liked* the man too, and she thought that he liked her. He had certainly acted as if he did, hadn't he? "Liked" was the operative word, though. He must think her an incurable klutz. She had tangled her wayward feet in wire at his cottage and then stumbled into his arms in the attic. It was getting to be a habit, albeit a rather pleasant one.

She was also struck by the feeling that in spite of the attraction between them he had some kind of barrier built up that hid his deepest thoughts. Even in those moments when he had held her closely, he had kept her at a distance. She could feel instinctively a reserve deep within him, something that kept him from anything more than a casual involvement.

Why wouldn't he feel that way? After all, he had good looks, charisma, a magnetic personality, and he traveled all over the world and no doubt met many sophisticated, beautiful women who could travel with him and laugh and love. . . .

"What on earth are you thinking about? You look as if you're ready to chew nails."

"Oh. Sorry, Dad." She groped for a plausible explanation and couldn't find one. "Just wondering what to have for dinner."

"The look in your eyes would probably poison anything you tried to fix. Let's order a large pepperoni and olive pizza."

She made herself smile, but could feel the smile waver just a little. "Okay. Sounds like a plan."

He sighed, watching her move around the workshop, her movements automatic and her mind obviously miles away. There was a dejected slope to her shoulders.

He had a pretty shrewd idea of what had been upsetting her these past few weeks. There wasn't much he could do about it except feel guilty, and to hope that he would not be a burden to her forever. She had a right to a life of her own.

Closing his eyes, he fought the sea of fatigue and depression that wanted to pull him down into its depths.

It was getting harder and harder to stay afloat. Perhaps he should just let go.

Louise called three days later.

She told Jenny she had cabin fever. Jenny managed not to laugh out loud: Louise's ornate Italianate mansion was a far cry from a cabin.

The doctor had told Louise she could get up, but she couldn't drive. If it wasn't too much trouble, she asked in her gracious and precise way, she wanted to come see Jenny and her father and all the projects and room boxes. Bennet had a meeting in Springfield the next day. He could drop her off and pick her up on the way back. She would be there about one, if that was all right.

Of course it was all right, but Jenny fought a strange pang of emotion that fell somewhere between relief and disappointment. So Bennet wouldn't be staying. Realistically, wasn't that just as well?

She knew Dad would enjoy the visit. It would give him something to think about besides the impending visit to Boston. His spirits were low. He was worrying about the results, and so was she.

Precisely at one, Louise appeared at the Blakemores' door with a solicitous Bennet at her elbow and an elegant cane with an ivory dog's-head handle in her hand. Bennet stayed only a few short minutes, but Jenny was keenly aware of the warmth in his eyes when he looked at her during the flurry of introductions and small talk between Louise and George. Or was she indulging in a childish bout of wishful thinking?

She walked back to the front door with him, leaving Dad and Louise in the workshop, both of them totally engrossed and chattering away happily like old friends.

"She's like a kid at Disneyland," Bennet said in a low voice. "Thank you for having her. Frankly, she's been driving me nuts the last few days."

Jenny chuckled. "It'll be good for her and Dad both. And Dad and I both enjoy showing off our work. Genuine appreciation is so good for the ego."

He hesitated for a moment, turning toward her. "Don't I know it." He smiled down at her wryly. "Jenny. . . ." There were warm pools of light deep in his dark eyes, and for a moment she thought he was going to kiss her. A traitorous tremor ran like a warm current through her blood, making her feel dizzy.

But he turned from her with a small shake of his head. "One of these days," he said cryptically. "One of these days. Soon." And he left her standing uncertainly on the top step of the porch, looking after him with questions buzzing through her mind like a swarm of confused bees.

Louise's visit was an unqualified success. She loved Gillyflower, she adored Merry Manor, she admired each and every room box and asked unending and intelligent questions.

Jenny could tell George liked her. The dark fog that had enveloped him lately thinned and almost disappeared as he answered questions and talked about Birney House.

The afternoon went so well, and so quickly, that Jenny was surprised and nearly disappointed to hear

Bennet's steps on the front porch as the sunlight began to fade behind the hills.

He was preoccupied, almost brusque. He wouldn't stay for a cup of coffee, saying he had some calls to make. The quick sideways smile he gave Jenny when he shepherded Louise out the front door seemed nothing but an afterthought to Jenny, and she felt a little hurt. It was just more evidence that she didn't know the man at all.

Louise waved at Jenny and George after she was settled in Bennet's van, then frowned slightly at her son.

"You were a bit rude just then, Bennet."

"Sorry." He studied the street ahead, his frown mirroring hers. He hadn't meant to sound rude, although he had certainly had a rotten afternoon. "I've got a problem with some major funding. I'll probably have to make a trip to the West Coast soon to get things squared away." He took a deep breath and glanced over at his mother. "But it'll work out—things always do. Did you have a good time?"

"Yes, of course. Jenny is so organized, and she works so exactingly. There is hardly a speck of dust in that workroom. And she and her father do such beautiful work, everything so neat and perfect. . . ."

"I know, I know. Are you making mental comparisons again?" He was amused in spite of himself.

"Well, dear, I do know you pretty well by now. Neatness is not one of your many virtues."

"But I'm lovable anyway."

"Yes." Louise studied her hands with evident absorption. "I wonder about her father." Bennet knew that this change of subject wasn't that at all, but was tied in closely with his self-admitted lovableness. "He is such a nice person. But I really can't see why his condition has persisted for so long. She has quite a job on her hands, taking care of him."

Bennet didn't answer. He knew that fact only too well.

"It just seems a little odd, I think," Louise went on thoughtfully. "There is something there that I cannot put my finger on. A look about the man, perhaps. I hope that the doctors can help him. Jenny is such a lovely young woman."

"Yes, she is," Bennet replied, swinging onto the main highway outside of Wellston, unaware that something in his tone of voice had brought a self-satisfied smile to his mother's face.

The specialist in Boston wanted Dad to stay for three days for a complete checkup, so Jenny made reservations at a hotel near the clinic. Getting away for a few days was a good idea, and she wanted to be with Dad during what would probably be an ordeal.

She called to let Louise know she would be out of town and to tell her that the shell of Birney House was cut and ready for assembly.

"I am so glad," Louise said thoughtfully. "Both that your father is going to get a thorough checkup and that Birney House has been started. I have heard of that group of doctors. They have an excellent success rate. I'm sure they'll find some way to help him."

Liz wasn't so confident. She frowned and fell silent for a few moments when Jenny told her about the trip. "You just can't believe a thing these doctors say," she finally muttered, looking resentful. Then she gave Jenny one of her bright smiles and said she hoped it would work out.

Over the next few days Liz didn't come over as often as usual, and Jenny decided she was brooding a little. *She hates to let him out of her sight*. The thought amused and touched her.

"I'll miss him—miss you both," Liz told her on the morning Jenny packed up the van for the trip. "In a way, I wish you weren't going. They haven't done much for him so far, have they? Actually, I think *I* can take care of him better than they can."

"Maybe this time things will be different," Jenny said with forced cheerfulness. Secretly, she shared Liz's misgivings, though not for the same reasons. But like a small, bright bird struggling for flight, hope was all that they had. It had to work.

"Of course you have to try. Have a safe trip. I'll see you when you get back."

Jenny felt marginally better by Thursday afternoon, when she had checked Dad into the hospital clinic. Dr. Berrigan, who had treated him after the accident, was there to talk to them both. Dad had begun to feel more like himself the last few days. No doubt, Jenny thought, because he knew he was going to get help, and his old natural optimism was taking over. It was infectious, making her feel more positive too.

The doctor was assured and efficient, and she knew

they would do their best. Jenny could only pray that it would be good enough. Dad would get round-the-clock monitoring, dozens of tests. . . . Of course they'd come up with something.

By five she was back in her motel room, wondering what to do to pass the evening. Dr. Berrigan had suggested that she come back about ten the next morning, allowing some time for early tests and evaluations. Jenny had two books and a deck of cards so that she could play solitaire—and a bad case of nerves, in spite of her guarded optimism.

When the phone rang at five-thirty she nearly jumped out of her skin. Had the doctors already found something terribly wrong with Dad? Who else would be calling her here? When she answered her "hello" was barely more than a squeak.

"Jenny? Is that you?"

"Bennet?" She sat down hard on the edge of the bed, trying to clear both her thoughts and her voice. It didn't work very well, and her next words sounded distinctly ungracious. "Why on earth are you calling me here? How did you even know where I was?"

"Mum told me. Talk about a warm reception. 'Gee, Bennet, it's good to hear from you.' I'm calling you because I wanted to. I'm in Boston until tomorrow afternoon. It's almost dinnertime. I'm hungry and I don't want to eat alone. I thought maybe you'd like some company, but maybe I was wrong. Do you have to go back to the clinic tonight? If you can manage to stand my company, I could go with you and give you some moral support if you need it."

Her heart melted. Darn the man. Bless the man. "Thank you," she answered softly. "I won't be going back to the clinic tonight, but it's been a long day, and I just realized that I could eat a horse."

"I didn't actually have a horse in mind. But I do know a place where we can get great seafood, ribs, or chicken. Even baked beans, if you want them. Shall I pick you up at seven?"

"Seven is fine." Jenny said good-bye and put down the phone. She sat dreamily staring into space for a few minutes, then tried to pull her thoughts back into order. What on earth was she going to wear? She really hadn't packed for anything like this.

Don't be silly, she told herself. *This isn't an inaugural ball. Bennet is just being thoughtful. It doesn't mean a thing. It's just a spur-of-the-moment dinner invitation.*

But she was into the shower and soaking wet before she remembered to take off her glasses.

In the end, she decided on her good brown wool skirt, the heathery tan V-neck sweater, and her vermilion turtleneck. It was a chilly evening, and her tweed jacket would feel good.

All that wonderful practicality left her feeling considerably less than glamorous. She blinked through her glasses, studying herself in the mirror. She looked like the stereotype of an old-fashioned librarian.

Well, it couldn't be helped, could it? She hadn't brought anything slinky with her. She didn't even own anything slinky, come to think of it. After all, she didn't want to look like a sex kitten, did she?

She dived suddenly for her traveling case. Eureka! A treasure she had forgotten about was in the side compartment. She had stashed a chunky, eye-catching hammered brass-and-copper necklace and matching earrings, in there during a trip to a three-day miniature show months ago.

She grabbed at the unruly mass of her hair and brushed it until, defeated, it obeyed her will and allowed itself to be swirled into a complicated concoction at the back of her head, intertwined with the vivid scarf she usually wore with the sweater. By the time she had spent twenty minutes on makeup that seemed invisible but made her glow, she decided she had done passably well with next to nothing.

At exactly six-fifty, she plopped down on the bench in front of the big dressing-table mirror and propped her chin in her hands, studying herself with a frown. For the first time in years she wished she could wear contact lenses. But she couldn't tolerate them.

Why such a flurry of attempted beautification, as if all this really mattered? Because, she assured herself, it took her mind away from fretting over Dad and it was good for her self-respect. But there was more to it than that.

The frantic activity had her heart pounding. A rosy, natural flush spread under the light blush she had applied to her cheekbones, bringing a brilliance that danced irrepressibly in her eyes.

No, she told the image in the mirror, *it's not the*

activity that is doing it. It's the fact that Bennet's going to be knocking at the door momentarily, and I mustn't let myself care so much. But she did care. She was caring more and more as time went by. And a reality check told her clearly that caring too much could put her in what was essentially a hopeless situation.

Some of the brilliance had faded from her eyes when Bennet rapped at the door. But he didn't know the glow had diminished. To him, the bright vision that looked up at him was a flame of sophisticated femininity that seared right into his heart, from her smile to her wonderful coppery hair to the flecks of green light in those sparkling eyes.

"Hey," he said, "you look smashing. I was looking for a redhead by the name of Jennifer Blakemore, but you'll do. You'll do just fine. How about spending a little time with me?"

"Well, now." Jenny reached up and straightened his pin-striped tie and flicked an imaginary speck from the lapel of his gray sports jacket, then tilted her head to give him a mock coy look. "If you're that famous documentary filmmaker Bennet Young, and I think you are, I couldn't pass that up for the world."

He chuckled. "You look great, Jenny, and we have twenty minutes to get to O'Boyle's. Ready?" He took her hand in his large tanned one and led her briskly and companionably down the long hotel hallway to the exit.

Watch out, Jenny, she told herself as he settled her into the beautiful, immaculate, red Corvette that awaited them. Red Corvette? Immaculate?

"Where did you get *this?*" she asked incredulously. Here was the red sports car she had envisioned when she first met him. It wasn't part of a dream after all.

He chuckled. "I've had it for years. It's a classic—I did most of the restoration myself. It's kept in the carriage house behind Mother's. I use the van most of the time, of course."

"Impressive." Well, it was. And he sounded so proud of it, which he should be. The man was full of surprises, wasn't he?

"Thank you. How's your father doing?"

"Settling in. I'm going back to the clinic tomorrow morning. They've started on early evaluations already."

"I hope they can do something for him."

"So do I. If he could just be completely independent. . . ." Her voice trailed off, and Bennet nodded, looking thoughtful. "For his sake," she added.

"Of course. And for yours."

And, he added to himself reluctantly and slightly ruefully as he pulled into the parking lot at the restaurant, *for mine, so you'd have more time for me.*

But that wasn't a thought he could realistically entertain, was it?

O'Boyle's turned out to be a sprawling, multiroom, dimly lit maze of dining and drinking and dancing areas encased in acres of dark oak woodwork and illuminated by vintage stained glass lamps.

The staff at O'Boyle's knew Bennet and seemed very glad to see him. The headwaiter led them to a small area near the dance floor. A patterned lamp on the table sent subdued jeweled pools of light over a white tablecloth.

The fact that they were in a public restaurant, doing something as commonplace as ordering a dinner, brought a thin veneer of calm to Jenny's mind. They ordered, talked of neutral things, ate dinner, and smiled readily and often at each other. And when the coffee came and soft, slow music filled the area and other couples got up to dance, they did too. The shell of calm dissolved the minute she was in his arms.

Closeness was inevitable, given the size of the dance floor and the number of couples on it. But even if they had been the only ones on the floor, they would have been wrapped inescapably in the intense magnetic field that brought them together.

For now, it was enough—the movement, the music, the nearness of this man who had walked right into her heart when she wasn't looking. They moved together through songs that came from somewhere inside of them, and the world disappeared.

At last there was a slight pause in the music. Bennet looked down at the top of her head and felt a stirring of sadness mixed with tenderness that grew and welled through him in a wave of regret.

He wanted to keep her like this forever, but he couldn't, could he? There were too many obstacles in the way. He couldn't allow himself to care this much. He had his responsibilities and she had hers, and they would inevitably separate them far too much.

A small voice that told him he didn't have to make

long-term commitments teased at the edges of his thoughts. Well, that was true. He could enjoy the moment. But he led her gently back to the table, unwilling to risk that physical closeness any longer.

The waiter refilled their coffee cups, and Jenny gave Bennet a slightly wavering smile over the edge of hers. "How long are you staying in Boston?" she asked, fighting back the disappointment that knifed through her with the realization that they couldn't keep dancing forever.

"Just until tomorrow afternoon. And you?"

"Three days of tests. Maybe they'll find something. It's a helpless feeling. . . ."

"You've done all you can. You can't keep feeling guilty."

"It's not guilt," she said defensively. "It's—I don't know. Fear. Frustration. Oh, I'm sorry. I shouldn't be so negative."

"No, you shouldn't." He said it more sharply than he had intended, and he stirred restlessly in his seat, unwilling to look her in the eye. He tried to soften his tone, but even to his own ears his next words were critical. "I think you take too much on yourself, you know."

"What else am I supposed to do? Stick him in a nursing home, leave him alone, not care about him?" Her voice had hardened, and when he glanced quickly at her, he wasn't surprised to see a familiar tilt to her chin and an angry spark in her eyes.

He was treading on thin ice. He hadn't intended to make her angry, or had he? Was it a defensive move on his part to put some kind of mental barrier between them? But that was ridiculous. He was dealing with a problem of his own: He cared too much about her, and this whole thing was a no-win situation.

He met her eyes at last. "It's my turn to apologize. I *am* sorry, Jenny. I worry about Mother when I have to be away, and she's certainly a lot more independent than your father is. You have reason to be concerned."

"Thank you. I shall continue being concerned, with your permission." The hard, icy edge to her voice had melted away and there was even a hint of a smile behind the words.

"Maybe I'm just a tiny bit jealous." He hadn't meant to say that, although he realized it was true. "Your brand of loyalty is hard to come by."

There was a moment's silence, and then she reached across the table and put her hand lightly on his. "That was sweet, you know that?"

"I'm never sweet," he protested. "Just ask anyone who has to work with me." But he knew his pleasure at her words showed in his voice. The woman was so uncannily skillful at making him feel things he didn't want to feel. Did she know what she was doing?

She looked at him levelly for a few minutes then sat back in her chair. "When will you be starting your film?"

"Preliminary work will start after the first of the year. Then we'll do a lot of the serious filming in spring and early summer."

"You'll be gone for quite awhile."

"That's the way it usually works out." He hesitated,

but not for long. "I wish you could come with me." Once again he was surprised at his own words, though, once again, they were true. He had wished that with Cheryl too. But Cheryl wouldn't travel with him, and Jenny couldn't.

Jenny blinked at him, coloring a little. His words had surprised her too. "That would probably be very interesting," she managed.

"It certainly would."

He was just teasing, wasn't he? Jenny took a deep breath and looked down at her watch. "I should get back," she said, much too brightly. "I have to be up early tomorrow."

"I understand." He did too, but that Machiavellian small voice that had earlier recommended a short-term involvement was whispering devilishly in the back of his mind.

"On the other hand," he said slowly, "I'm staying at the Ritz-Carlton. Maybe we could stop off there and have a nightcap."

"I don't think so, Bennet." One eyebrow was raised, and he knew she was aware of exactly what was going through his mind. He should probably apologize.

"Sorry," he said. But he left her to figure out whether he was sorry he asked or sorry she had said no.

They drove back to her motel in comfortable silence. He kissed her good night outside her door.

"I'll be in touch, love," he told her. "Sleep well."

He disappeared down the hall, and she slipped inside

her room, shut the door, and leaned against it, closing her eyes tightly.

Where had that ridiculous tear come from? She took off her glasses and dashed it away impatiently, only to have another take its place.

Sleeping well was not something she would be able to do tonight.

There was no call from Bennet the next morning. She didn't know whether she was relieved or disappointed. And there was no news from the doctors, only vague reassurances. Dad smiled at her with forced cheerfulness when she walked in the door, but she could see the hopelessness in his eyes.

Nor was there anything more than vague reassurances over the next few days. Jenny spent as much time as she could with her father, hoping for a breakthrough, her mind caught up in an endless tangle of thoughts of the future and of Bennet.

''He is definitely depressed,'' she was told on the second day. ''That may be slowing the healing. Still, it's hard to tell.''

On the third day there was nothing more, nothing concrete, no magic pink pills. They did have some medication they wanted him to try. It could help.

''And try to keep him busy. Keep up his spirits, if you can,'' one of the psychologists told her.

It would be easier to do that if her own spirits weren't dragging along in a bottomless canyon, but she could try. She had to try.

On the drive back to Wellston, she pointed out everything from pumpkins in the fields to the amazing number of small red sports cars on the road—an observation that had meaning for her as well.

But nothing worked. Dad's silence was almost unbroken, although toward the end of the trip he sighed and said it would be good to be home again.

Jenny didn't like the way he said it. It sounded as if he were going home to die.

Jenny's own depression deepened with each mile. There was uneasiness and concern about Dad, and something more there too. It was more than even the hopeless feeling she had when she thought about Bennet.

Jenny wasn't sure she believed in premonitions, but the closer they got to Wellston, the more she felt something was wrong. But of course that was ridiculous; what could go wrong in a peaceful small town in three or four days? Liz had been keeping an eye on things, and Jenny was just being silly.

Everything looked perfectly normal when she pulled into their driveway. It seemed as if the house were welcoming them home, mutely saying it was glad they were back. She had been worried about nothing.

It took awhile to get Dad comfortable and to put on a pot of coffee for the two of them, then she wrestled their bags from her van and stashed them away. Tomorrow she would take care of all that. For now, it was just good to be back.

It was half an hour before she had put their dishes in the dishwasher and wandered out to the workshop to pick up the pieces of the small cabinet Dad had been working on before they left. It needed another sanding, and that would keep his hands busy for a while.

She knew what had happened even before she walked through the door into the dusky light of the workroom. The emptiness made itself felt by the time she flipped the light switch and stood in horror in the doorway.

The glass was broken out of the wide door on the far side of the workroom. Sharp pieces caught the last of the afternoon light at the window itself, and shards were scattered in front of it.

The big workbench was empty. Gillyflower Cottage was gone.

Chapter Eight

Jenny didn't scream, nor did she pound the walls. She didn't break into tears—although she wanted to—and she didn't quite panic.

But by the next afternoon she felt as if she had done all those things and more. Her well of emotional reserves was drained dry and exhaustion had left her in a trancelike state. All those months of work—lost.

She had managed to call the police, and she broke the news to Dad as gently as she could. His initial reaction was to grow even paler than before, which hurt her almost as much as the theft. But then, to Jenny's surprise, he rallied. Anger took the place of shock and gave him strength.

The police officer who came to make the report was kind but not particularly encouraging. Had anything else been taken? What was the value of the dollhouse? He shook his head and stared at her in disbelief when she told him.

Jenny called Liz almost as soon as the police. Liz would be the most likely person to have seen anything strange.

"Oh, Jenny. Oh, George. No, I didn't see anything. I brought the mail in twice, but I just left it on the hall table, and I didn't go through to the workshop." Liz's face was pale and she looked ready to break into tears herself. "Wouldn't they have used a van to get Gillyflower away from here? I didn't see one. And I certainly didn't let your house key out of my sight, honest I didn't. Oh, Jenny. I'm so sorry."

Jenny had to steel herself to try to cheer up her neighbor, and vaguely resented it. She had to be the pillar of strength for Dad and Liz when her own nerves felt like a mass of soggy day-old spaghetti.

Nothing else was missing, which was strange. This meant that Liz could say, in an effort to cheer her up, "It could have been so much worse, dear."

That thought made neither Jenny nor George feel much comforted.

She would have to call the writer in Salem who had commissioned Gillyflower. She dreaded that, so she decided to put it off for a few days while the police checked things out. Maybe the whole episode was just a prank, and Gillyflower would turn up inside the library or the town hall or out behind Mr. MacGruder's barn.

Several times Jenny had a sneaky, absurd desire to run to Bennet and cry on his broad shoulder. But her relationship with him was complicated enough already. She felt instinctively that while crying on his shoulder might make her feel better, it would make her feel worse in the long run. So she stayed close to Dad during the following day, double-checked the house, and talked to the neighbors across the street and to the police and tried to make sense out of the whole thing. But it just wasn't possible.

Dad looked over their original list of supplies for Gillyflower after the news broadcast that evening. "I suppose we should start rounding up the raw materials again," he announced. "The sooner the better."

She looked up at him with a touch of surprise. He didn't exactly sound enthusiastic, but he sounded better than *she* felt—more positive, at least.

"Starting over," she mused, knowing her voice betrayed her own depression. "It's so hard. Right now, I don't know whether I can build Gillyflower all over again."

"Well, of course you can. Of course *we* can."

She studied him closely. "You almost sound as if you feel better. Is that new medication helping?"

He frowned slightly, thinking it over. "I'm not sure what it is, Jenny. I know the doctors didn't come up with anything helpful, and that did get me down at first. But physically I think the few days away did me some good."

"I'm so glad." She hoped it would continue. "You go ahead and make a list of what we'll need. I'd better call Louise and tell her we'll probably be delayed starting on Birney House."

Unexpectedly, Bennet answered the phone—in a gruff, impatient way—when she called. His voice sent an involuntary shiver tingling across Jenny's nerve endings.

"Bennet? What on earth are you doing there? This is Jenny."

"I know," he said wryly, "And I'm so glad you're filled with joy at hearing my voice. I'm playing electrician again since nothing in the kitchen seems to work. Mother's taking a rest, it's Mrs. Huckaby's day off, and I was closest to the phone. I suppose you actually wanted to talk to Mum, since you sounded unpleasantly surprised to hear me answer." Then his voice softened. "How's your dad?"

"I'm sorry, Bennet. I was just surprised when you picked up the phone." She could hear the caressing note in her own voice and tried to swallow it. She was trying so hard to feel neutral about this man, and it was impossible. "Dad is a little bit better. I actually called to tell Louise that we're going to be unavoidably delayed in starting on Birney House." A wobble had replaced the caress in her voice, and Bennet reacted to it immediately with soft, probing questions that very nearly caused a storm of tears.

Explaining the theft over the phone wasn't nearly as satisfying as burying her head in his chest and sobbing it all out, but still it helped. He was indignant, he was gentle, he was sympathetic—he said all the right things.

"Mum will be disappointed, of course. But she'll be furious at whoever did it, and worried about you and your father. It's really weird that the crooks didn't take anything but Gillyflower, isn't it?"

It was. The police had thought so too, which had immediately put suspicion on people who might have seen the cottage at the miniature shows. This was a thought that Jenny hated. Miniaturists were her friends and her customers, not thieves. It made her feel betrayed.

''And Mother wanted to talk to you too,'' he was saying. ''She has a bee in her bonnet about that old portrait of Susannah Hayes. She thinks she knows where it is. But maybe you don't want to think about anything to do with Birney House right now.''

''Oh, but I do.'' Jenny felt a stirring of excitement. Finding the painting would solve one mystery, anyway, and right now, she needed all the good news she could get. ''Does she think it's at Birney House?''

''Sounds that way. And I think she wants me to dismantle a wall. I don't suppose. . . .'' He hesitated for a moment, sounding uncharacteristically uncertain. ''I don't suppose you'd like to come up and help in the search?''

''I'd love to. When?'' She sounded too eager, but she just didn't care.

''Saturday?'' he suggested, laughing a little. ''I'm sure Mother would be glad to have both you and your father.''

''I'll see how he feels,'' she promised. When she hung up, she stood still for a few minutes, trying to sort out her cartwheeling emotions. She felt so much better having talked to Bennet, and at the same time, she knew her feelings about him were getting out of hand. It just wasn't a good sign. She was on an emotional roller coaster, and she didn't know how to stop it.

Dad hedged at making the trip with her. Not this time, he said, since he had some small projects to finish up before they restarted construction on Gillyflower. Maybe next time, he suggested optimistically, and that in itself was a surprise.

Jenny felt uneasy about how she should act on her next encounter with Bennet. It would be much easier if Louise came to Birney House with them. Then he wouldn't be so much of a temptation and maybe she could keep her emotions in check.

She felt that little prickle of tears behind her eyelids and blinked them back. She hadn't planned on falling in love with the man.

The thought, the admission, shook her to her toes. She retreated to her room and let the tears flow. She had been holding back for days, and now she allowed herself to drown in a torrent of self-pity and uncertainty and misery over everything: Dad's health, Gillyflower, Bennet.

How on earth was she ever going to get everything sorted out?

On Saturday a slow, cold drizzle put a further damper on her already low spirits, and she came close to calling off her trip. But she did want to share in the excitement of finding the lost portrait. And she did want to see Bennet again.

Liz stopped in on Saturday morning with a plate of brownies. "Oh, you just *have* to go," Liz said. "If you can find that picture—wouldn't it be exciting?"

"Go, Jenny. You need the break," George told her.

Liz stood beside him with one hand on his shoulder, nodding vehemently. "You certainly do, what with all that's happened. And I'll bring a snack over for your dad, and you don't have to worry about a thing."

Finally she agreed to go. Liz and George both beamed their approval.

"But do drive carefully in this awful rain," Liz told her in a low voice when they walked out on the porch. The eaves were dripping more heavily now, and the chill in the air spoke of the onset of winter.

"Don't worry. I'm used to driving in the rain," Jenny told Liz, touched at her concern.

"I suppose you'll see that nice-looking Bennet, won't you? You two do make such an attractive couple. You should be planning for the future, you know that?"

"Well, I—" Jenny started, but Liz cut her off.

"You mustn't worry so about your father. I can always help take care of him, after all. And you have your life to live—I'm interfering, aren't I? Sorry, Jenny. Have a good time this afternoon." Liz hurried away, splashing across the puddles between the houses, leaving Jenny standing with a bemused smile and shaking her head. Liz made things sound so easy.

But still, a sense of anticipation began to glow like her own private ray of sunlight as Jenny drove up the long drive toward Louise's mansion. *Enjoy the moment,* she told herself. *Maybe things are going to get better now. . . .*

She gave Caesar a friendly pat. Damp and dejected, he was sprawled over half the entry porch. He managed a reluctant thump of the tail and eyed her morosely, then stared at the front door with a gleam of hope.

"I don't think so," she told him. "You're too big and too wet to be allowed in the house." He groaned and put his massive head back on his paws at the same time that Mrs. Huckaby opened the door.

"We've been watching for you. She's waiting for you in the east parlor," Mrs. Huckaby greeted her abruptly. But she said it with a friendly smile that took any edge off the words. Jenny had the feeling that she had been accepted at last.

A fire burned in the marble fireplace that dominated the wall opposite the windows in the spacious room. Louise sat at her tea table, more than ready for scones and tea and talk. It was a room designed for those things: English chintzes and doors leading out to a garden, soft cushy furniture and country landscapes on the walls. Jenny sank into a chair opposite Louise with a sigh of near contentment. If Bennet had been there the contentment would have been complete.

Louise told her he was gathering his tools together and probably grabbing a ham and Swiss sandwich and a quart of milk in the kitchen. "He's not terribly fond of scones and tea," Louise explained with a sniff.

"But I *am* rather fond of Jenny," a voice said from the doorway. Jenny felt the color rise in her face and turned quickly to see him lounging against the door frame, watching her with a smile that made her toes tingle.

"Are you, dear? How nice. Come in and join us while Jenny tells me all about her father and the terrible theft of Gillyflower Cottage."

Jenny found it was difficult to speak coherently of those things with Bennet perched closely and casually on the broad arm of her overstuffed chair, but she managed well, she thought.

"Now, what about the portrait of Susannah?" she asked at last. "You know where she is?"

"I think so, but to prove it Bennet will have to dismantle the built-in bookshelves under a stairwell. You see, I remembered something my grandmother had told me when I was a child. Apparently Enoch Hayes's daughter-in-law had a running feud with Susannah during her lifetime."

"Probably just old family gossip," Bennet contributed skeptically. "But we'll take a look."

"There is usually a basis for old family gossip, Bennet," Louise told him. "Grandmother said that it ended with the portrait being put in the cubbyhole to keep the mice company. I suppose it must still be there. Under the stairs is the only place I can think of where that cubbyhole might be. I certainly hope there are no mice in it."

"I guess we'll find out," Bennet said. "Ready, Jenny?" He stood and held out a hand to help pull her to her feet. The warmth of his hand, his touch, was electrifying.

Jenny pulled her hand away with reluctance and reminded herself that she had intended to enjoy the moment. And at this particular moment, that was a dangerous thought.

Louise would wait here by the fire where she could be comfortable. She said her back still ached at times. From the gleam in Louise's eye, Jenny thought it more likely that she was playing her matchmaking game again, with an optimistic vision of the future.

On the porch, Bennet hesitated, looking at Caesar. "All right," he finally answered the imploring look in the dog's eyes. "You can come with us. But you'll have to stay in the kitchen at Birney House."

Caesar seemed to think this was an entirely acceptable idea, and he settled contentedly in the back of Bennet's van with a resigned sigh and later at the door that led to the cellar of the silent old home. He looked at them, looked at the door, and flopped onto his side.

"Good thing we don't want to go down into the cellar," Bennet said. "We'd have to climb over a dog-mountain."

"Where are the bookcases and the cubbyhole?" Jenny asked, not at all interested in the cellar. "Do you think we'll find anything?"

"Dust, probably," Bennet answered with a chuckle. He could tell that Jenny was trying to curb her excitement and enthusiasm. In the semidarkness of the large, low-ceilinged kitchen, her hair and eyes were glinting with that special, appealing electricity that he had seen before.

It felt so good to have her beside him, helping unload the waist-high cases that had been built in under the stairs. The staircase itself was one of the few structural changes that had been made in the house. The original stairs had been the narrow, half-hidden passage from the kitchen.

"I think they put this in around 1850," he told Jenny when he reached for the crowbar he had brought along, ''so there would be room for a pantry underneath at the back and storage under the stairs.''

''Until the bookcases were built,'' Jenny added. ''Can't you go any faster?''

He laughed at her impatience, then put all of his strength into dismantling the shelves. ''They certainly built these things to last,'' he grumbled. It was both a complaint and a compliment across the years to the carpenters who had worked so conscientiously one hundred and fifty years before.

With creaking and dust and a horrendous splintering of wood, the shelves gave way at last. And once he pried under the edges, parted reluctantly from the supporting studs.

Jenny sneezed twice at the billowing dust and then anxiously aimed the flashlight into the murky darkness under the stairs.

There were cobwebs and dust, and an old pair of moldering snowshoes, and what looked suspiciously like an old cracked chamberpot.

''There, back in the corner,'' she said breathlessly. ''Is that a frame? It's facing the wall, there at the left.'' She ducked her head and started forward, then encountered a tangled network of spiderwebs and pulled back, swiping at her face and muttering fiercely to herself. Bennet gathered she didn't much like spiders.

''I'll get it,'' he told her. He took the flashlight and managed to get his own head and shoulders into the narrow space under the stairs.

It *was* a picture. ''Got it,'' he said, and backed out, turning the frame as he emerged.

"That's it!" Jenny sounded awed, staring down at the portrait. It was grimy and the frame had a gouge at one side, but it definitely matched the frame surrounding old Enoch. For the first time in years, Susannah Hayes stared down a rather long nose, with a severe and imperious look in her eyes, out at the light of the world.

Jenny took her glasses off and polished them vigorously on her shirttail, then laid the glasses on a hall table and backed away, eyes narrowed, to squint at Susannah. "She looks as if she was a very strong person," she decided. "I'll bet they were quite a pair. What a face."

Bennet looked down at the picture and then up at Jenny, and then laughed softly as he reached out and brushed his fingers lightly across her cheeks. "What a face, all right," he murmured, his voice gentle and full of warmth. "A wonderful face, full of light and life and cobwebs."

For a moment he stood silent and still, etching a portrait of Jenny deep into his own mind where it could stay forever: a tiny flush across her cheekbones under the smudges, excitement in her eyes, and soft lips that needed to be kissed. Now.

And so he did, webs and all, arms gathering her so close that he could feel her tremble. A surge of tenderness made him give her lips a butterfly-light kiss with a power that shut out the rest of the world.

Her arms were around him, clinging fiercely, and then she turned her head with a strangled sob, resting her forehead on his chest, breathing raggedly, obviously, painfully, trying to break the spell.

He didn't want to break it. The magic that leaped into blazing life when they touched was something he wanted to keep forever.

"Jenny?"

"It's all right." There was a tear in her voice, and the sound drove a tiny dagger into his heart.

"It was more than all right. Oh, Jenny, don't cry. I wouldn't hurt you."

"I know that. Not on purpose, anyway." She sniffed, and from behind the tear came a chuckle. Their arms were still around each other, more loosely now, and he realized that they were swaying together, almost dancing in time with unheard music.

Then Jenny straightened her shoulders and back and stood very still, another inch away from him. "It won't work, Bennet. I care too much for you."

He could have laughed at the studied seriousness of her tone; the words would have sounded appropriate coming from the proper Susannah. But it wasn't a laughing matter. "But that's wonderful," he said. "Isn't it? Since I feel the same way, and I'd like to keep you near me forever. I'd like to take you to all the fabulous gardens of the world."

"Oh, Bennet, yes, and no. That's what I meant—it won't work."

"I don't see why not."

"I can't travel with you. I can't make any plans for the future until Dad's better."

"But we could work around that. We could hire a housekeeper for him."

"Bennet, listen. He would hate that."

He felt exasperated; he always did when he couldn't think of quick answers to a knotty problem. "So what do you think we should do?"

"Cool it." That was the one phrase he didn't want to hear, and there was a catch in her voice that told him she didn't really like the idea any better. "Let's give Dad a chance to get better. Then maybe, if you still want to work things out. . . ."

There was a long silence. Outside, the dismal rain drummed against the windows, and the last of the birch leaves slipped, sodden, to the ground. It promised to be a long, dark winter.

"Cruel woman." This wasn't going well, not at all. "I'll be gone for months at a time when spring comes."

"Maybe Dad will be better by then. And maybe he won't. Anyway, you'll be very busy. Maybe things will be different by the time you come back."

"That's a lot of maybes, and a long time." It could be forever, come to that. He didn't want to think about it.

"I know." She turned away from him, her shoulders and back no longer so straight, picked up her glasses and rubbed a furtive hand across her eyes before she put them back on. "For now, I think we'd better decide what to do about Susannah." Her voice wavered slightly.

He gave in, but, he told himself, only temporarily. He would marshal some persuasive arguments in the next few days. Somehow things could be worked out.

As for Susannah, they would take her to Louise, and he could make some repairs to the frame. He had to fix the shelves under the stairs now too. And then Susannah could be put back next to Enoch, where she belonged, just as Jenny belonged next to him.

They collected Caesar from the kitchen. He hadn't moved from his post at the cellar door, almost as if he had been standing guard—or, more accurately, *sleeping* guard. He thudded along beside them, head low, sensing their mood. Outside, he lifted his head and bayed at the tree branches, then padded, snuffling, along the side of the house, inspecting cellar windows for a few minutes before getting reluctantly into the van.

All the gray gloom of a cold, wet, late-fall afternoon wrapped itself around them as they drove back, not speaking, to give Louise the wonderful news that they had found Susannah.

If Louise wondered why they were so glum and despondent about their success in finding hidden treasure, she didn't let on. She showed enough enthusiasm and delight to make up for their near silence, but Jenny was keenly conscious of the quick, thoughtful looks Louise shot their way.

"Take the picture with you," Louise decided, "so that your friend can make a good miniature copy. While it does have value, I know that it will be in good hands."

The rain had turned to a depressing late-afternoon mist when Bennet watched Jenny drive away, trying to hold on to a shred of hope that things might work out. She was taking his heart with her too: It probably had some value; was it also in good hands?

He loved her. He knew that now. And the fact made him achingly vulnerable, which was a feeling that had long been foreign to him.

He gruffly ordered Louise to go take a rest (she smiled forgivingly at him, which made him feel worse), bundled a soggy Caesar into his van, and drove glumly back to the gatehouse to make his reservations for the trip to Los Angeles.

Ben Williams leaned back in the wobbly old folding chair and crossed his burly arms over his chest, staring at the small patch of tentative light coming through the grubby window in the coalhole.

This sort of thing couldn't be good for a man's heart. But he still didn't understand what was going on with that dog. He had been cowering down here in a corner of the cellar like an old lop-eared rabbit hiding in a berry patch, waiting for that long-haired monster to rumble him, and the dog hadn't let out a whine, much less a roar. Why not? He must have known Ben was there; dogs were darned smart that way. To top it off, the stupid animal had stared right into the coalhole window, looked straight into his eyes, and hadn't even blinked. Ben had thought his heart would stop beating at that moment. This was it. He was caught.

Then the dog had just turned and walked away. Just like that.

He remembered a dog he had owned when he was young—Skipper, a feisty little mutt. Skipper could tell friend from foe from half a mile away, and never barked at anyone who wasn't a threat. Maybe this dog was like that.

He got up and walked over to the high window, peering out at the dripping undergrowth that surrounded the foundations. It was lousy weather, and it was bound to get lousier as the weeks went by. Soon it would be snowing, and the people who lived here would be back, or that big dog would decide he was going to tell on him, or he would get snowed in . . .

His married daughter in Dayton would take him in. She probably didn't know what had happened to him over the past year; she probably thought he was dead. He wasn't sure how she would take to his walking in right out of the blue, but she had always been a good girl. She would let him stay for a while, just until he got on his feet, got a job.

If he went into town, got a few odd jobs, maybe he could save up enough for a bus ticket. If not, he could try hitchhiking, though he didn't like that idea much. It was better to save up the money. In the meantime, he could probably slip back here at night for a warm place to sleep.

It was a mighty good feeling to know that he was finally planning ahead, that he might be able to put his life back together.

Jenny found herself blinking back stinging tears several times on the way home, biting furiously at her lower lip, trying to think straight.

Had he even said he loved her? And was there a

commitment in the fact that he said he wanted to have her with him all the time? He hadn't mentioned anything about marriage, had he? She wouldn't go away with him unless they were married.

Marriage. She hadn't even thought of anything like that over the last few years. Besides, as she had told him, she couldn't think about any kind of a lasting relationship with him. Not at this point.

These thoughts chased themselves around in tight circles with no reason, no ending point, no purpose, no answers. It was no wonder that she felt dizzy and a little sick.

She felt relieved when she passed the Wellston town limits at last. She was almost home, and she would surely feel better once she had some dinner, a warm bath, a talk with Dad, a chance to return to what was familiar and normal.

But as she pulled into the driveway, an unwelcome prickle of intuition told her that things were not normal after all. Even though it was nearly dark, there was no glow of light from any of the windows. She pulled down the long drive toward the back of the house with a small frown. Even the workshop windows looked dark and cold.

Maybe Dad had fallen asleep. That must be the answer, she told herself as she jumped out of her van and hurried toward the back door. The thought, logical as it was, did nothing to chase away the needles of apprehension that were growing stronger with every second.

''Dad?'' she called as she opened the door and

flipped on the kitchen light switch. "Dad, where are you?"

No answer. There were a couple of coffee mugs neatly rinsed and drying on the counter next to the sink—apparently Liz had been over to visit. She glanced into the workshop and hurried toward the living room, flipping on lights all the way. No sign of him.

Panic began to rise in her throat. He couldn't be so soundly asleep that he couldn't hear her calling. His sleep these days was troubled, never that deep. . . .

His bedroom door was open halfway, and beyond it she could see the back of the wheelchair sitting askew at the end of the empty bed.

Then she saw his slipper, his foot. He was on the floor just beyond the wheelchair, motionless, sprawled crookedly with arms outstretched, as if reaching for help.

For a moment, as the light brought the scene into startling reality, Jenny grasped the door frame and stood stock still, trying not to slip helplessly to the floor.

She thought she screamed, but she wasn't certain. Nothing seemed real. It couldn't be. "Dad?" she asked on a sob, but knew that he couldn't answer.

Trembling from head to toe, she crossed the room and fell to her knees beside him.

Chapter Nine

She ran her fingers across his forehead. He was warm yet clammy and unresponsive. She pressed a trembling hand to his neck. He did have a pulse—weak and rapid, but he was alive.

Had he tried to get into bed, and fallen? Had he passed out? She started to put her arm under him to turn him, then stopped. What if he was injured? And his breathing was so shallow—she suspected he needed oxygen.

For the next several minutes, time expanded and contracted in uneven pulses of activity. She managed to get hold of the emergency room at the small local hospital. They would send an ambulance out immediately. They told her to try to make him comfortable.

He had turned from his stomach to his side by the time she hung up, and she grabbed a pillow to slip under his head. His eyelids fluttered slightly and she thought he knew she was there, that he was trying to speak, and she tried to soothe him.

And then she heard the welcome wail of the siren, and released him into other, more professional, hands.

Her own trembling had stopped now, but a disquieting whisper of guilt nagged at her. If she had been here, if she hadn't been spending those precious moments with Bennet. . . .

Putting those thoughts out of her mind as best she could, she answered the questions about the presence of the wheelchair, his state of health, his medications. She followed the stretcher out to the ambulance, barely conscious of the curious and concerned neighbors who had gathered up and down the block to watch in spite of the chilly, damp evening.

Liz stood on the sidewalk, pale and wild-eyed, asking questions that Jenny didn't have answers to.

"I'll let you know as soon as I know anything," she told Liz. "I'm going to follow the ambulance to the hospital."

"Would you like me to go with you?"

"No," she answered so quickly and so sharply that she was almost sorry as soon as the word came out. But she didn't need or want Liz with her. "They'll probably only allow immediate family near him, Liz," she said more kindly.

There were tears on Liz's cheeks, or perhaps it was the rain, which had started up again in earnest. "I'll wait until I hear from you, then," she told Jenny, and then turned and trudged disconsolately back to her own house.

The next few hours were interminable. Jenny sat in the emergency waiting area, aware of other strained faces and nervous voices, feeling surrounded and overwhelmed by the fear and uncertainty around her. The soothing or matter-of-fact or sympathetic voices of the doctors and nurses could have been part of an old movie with a distorted sound track. This was all a dream. It had to all be a nightmare, and soon she would wake up.

At last a young doctor approached her, smiling a little, eyes gentle. "Jenny Blakemore?" he asked. She nodded numbly. "I'm Dr. Rothke. He's not in any danger now. We're taking him up to a room. It would be a good idea for you to fill out all the necessary paperwork at the front desk, and by that time they can tell you which room he's in. And I'd like to talk to you later, of course, when we get him settled in."

"Of course." There was something about this man that she liked—a sharp intelligence in his eyes, a deep compassion. She felt comforted.

Later they allowed her to sit beside her father's bed, and she held his hand and talked to him for a short time.

All he managed to say was, "I'm so sorry. I don't know what happened. I just felt so sick, so dizzy. . . ."

She told him that he would be all right now, he mustn't be sorry, everything would be fine, and she tried very hard to believe it. When a nurse slipped in and suggested that Jenny go home and get some rest, she could only agree reluctantly. She felt empty, emotionally and physically wrung out, and Dad would sleep now. It was hard to believe it was after two in the morning.

As tired as she was, she was unable to relax completely when she got home. She ate half a sandwich, drank half a glass of milk, paced the house for a while, took a shower, fell into bed, and lay staring at the moon shadows on the window. The rain had stopped. Perhaps tomorrow things would look better.

What next? she wondered as a jumble of thoughts gathered at the edge of the downward slope to an uneasy sleep. Gillyflower missing, her deep, unconquerable attraction to Bennet, and now Dad. . . .

Her thoughts swirled and blurred together, and she slept at last.

Jenny was up again by seven, bleary-eyed and weary. She called the hospital. She was told George had rested well, and Dr. Rothke wanted to talk to her when she came in. She tried to ignore the ominous sound to the doctor's request.

She choked down breakfast cereal that tasted like straw, drank a glass of orange juice, and slipped into her gray skirt, a heathery-gray tunic top, and her brightest scarf, which might lift Dad's spirits—if not her own. She was almost out of the front door when she remembered belatedly to report back to Liz.

Liz answered the phone on the first ring, as if she had been waiting. "I hardly slept last night, I was worrying so much," Liz told her. "You call me back when you know more, hear? Do they have any idea yet what caused it all?" The strain of anxiety in her neighbor's voice was contagious.

"I don't know. I'm going to talk to the doctor this morning."

"You give your dad my love. We just wouldn't want anything to happen to him, would we?"

It seemed to Jenny that something had already happened, but she managed to thank Liz for her concern before she raced out the door.

She found her father sitting up in bed, watching for her, a glass of apple juice on his tray. His color looked better. "They won't let me eat anything solid, since my stomach was so upset last night," he explained. It was a relief to note a mild tone of complaint in the words.

"Have you talked to Dr. Rothke?"

"He was in for a short time. He said he'd have to know a lot more before he knew anything at all. He asked me if I suffered from allergic reactions."

"Well, that's an interesting thought."

"I thought so too," a voice from the doorway said. "But it's just a shot in the dark at this point." Dr. Rothke strode across the room and stood looking down at George thoughtfully. "You're a puzzle," he told him. "So right now, the best thing you can do is rest."

"I guess that's an invitation for me to leave for a while," Jenny said. She didn't want to. At this point she hardly wanted to let Dad out of her sight, even though he was safe.

"I'd like to talk to you, if you don't mind," Dr. Rothke told Jenny. "We can use the chapel lounge—it's quiet."

He had the kind of straight-on manner that left little room for argument. Jenny squeezed her father's shoulder and gave him a kiss on the forehead, then followed the doctor.

Once they were settled in the lounge, Dr. Rothke leaned forward with clipboard on his knee and asked lots of questions—about the accident, the clinic's evaluations, George's medications and diet.

"You don't mind if I call the clinic in Boston for more information? It could be crucial."

"Of course not," Jenny told him. "But what do you think happened to him? He's never had a spell like this before."

Dr. Rothke leaned back and studied the wall behind her head. "I could only guess, at this point. And guesses aren't good enough. The main thing is that he's better this morning, but I don't want him to go home until I've checked his full medical history and had a chance to observe him. You'll be available, I assume."

"Of course I will. I wouldn't leave him alone at a time like this."

"You can believe that," a voice behind her said. Jenny's heart jumped into her throat and she turned to see Bennet standing in the lounge doorway. "She sticks to her father like warm glue," he continued.

"Bennet!" She blinked, taking her glasses off and putting them back on again as if to verify that he wasn't a stray reflection on the lenses. "How on earth did you know where I was? What are you doing here?"

"I'll explain it all later." Bennet looked at the doctor with a hint of a smile. "I'm Bennet Young, a family friend," he told the doctor.

"I'm Dr. Rothke," the doctor replied. "Come in and join us. I think Jenny could use a family friend right now."

Bennet crossed the floor under the searching gaze of the doctor, coming to sit beside her on the small sofa, draping his arm casually but protectively across her shoulders. It felt so good to have him there beside her. "How are you holding up?" he asked, his voice low. Jenny leaned against him, temporarily unable to speak.

"I'll leave you two, then," Dr. Rothke said, rising. "I think I have all the information I need right now. I want to do a couple of tests and talk to Mr. Blakemore. You might as well get some lunch and come back to see him a little later."

When he was out of the room, Jenny sagged a little. The nightmarish part was over, but it still seemed like an unreal dream.

"It's been awful," she whispered. Then she sat up straight, looking questioningly at Bennet. "You still haven't told me how you knew."

He hesitated for a moment. Actually, full of frustration, love, and a need to let Jenny know how much he cared for her, he had driven down to tell her that he understood, and that he would wait as long as necessary for her father to regain his health, that he would be there for her, no matter what.

But this wasn't an auspicious time to talk about her dad's health. Declaring undying love probably could wait for a better time too, sometime when she had less on her mind and he could prove he was telling the truth. But he could at least let her know that he was here for her—until he had to take off on some journey or other. He sighed. This was still a no-win situation.

"I just needed to see you today, I guess. Yesterday was kind of hard on both of us. Anyway, Liz met me before I even got out of my car and told me your dad was in the hospital. I still don't know what happened."

"Nobody does. And I don't know how long it'll be. . . ."

"I know. Look, I'm here, and I'll stay with you. Let's go to the Herb Garden for lunch. It's not far, and you look as if you could use soup or an omelet or at least a cup of herb tea."

"Thank you," she said simply. "I think I'd like the company. And the herb tea too."

Slipping into one of the comfortable booths at the Herb Garden, Jenny gave a deep sigh. Coping with all of this alone would have been so much harder. She was used to being the care giver. Having someone taking care of her was such a strange experience. And it felt so good.

They ordered omelets and salads, and Bennet watched her closely as if he were afraid she might self-destruct.

"You're doing okay?" he asked, reaching across to take her hand.

"I think so."

"He's in good hands."

"I know. It would be wonderful if Dr. Rothke could find some hint of what's wrong." She looked up at him and managed a smile. "Thank you for being here."

"I'd like to make a habit of it, you know."

She shook her head slightly. "Except, of course, for when you have to be gone."

There was no reproach or bitterness in her voice, only resignation, and it was his turn for a deep sigh. He released her hand and leaned back, unable to restrain the slight twinge of guilt that caught at his mind.

"I have to be gone all next week, I'm afraid." How he wished this trip wasn't so important. Momentarily he thought of postponing it, but it was too late for that. "I'll be catching a plane to Los Angeles tomorrow evening. But I'll come by the hospital before I go to see you both. And I'll call every day, if you don't mind."

Very quietly, after a moment's hesitation, she said, "I'll miss you, Bennet. A lot."

There was a quality in her voice that spoke volumes more than the simple words conveyed. He felt a lump in his throat, and lifted her hand to his lips and kissed it, not caring who might see the old-fashioned gesture.

"Jenny, I love you," he heard himself mumble hoarsely. He knew it was true, but he hadn't intended to say it right at this moment. He cleared his throat and said it more succinctly—with intensity, with feeling. "Jenny Blakemore, I love you very much."

She stared at him, her eyes shining brightly behind the protection of her glasses. It wasn't enough protection to keep him from knowing that the brightness came from unshed, happy tears.

"And I love you back, just as much," she said with a quaver in her voice. "Too much, maybe. Is that good or bad?"

"More tea?" the middle-aged waitress asked. And then, in embarrassed surprise, "Oh! Sorry. I can come back in a few minutes, if you'd rather."

Since they didn't answer or even know she was there, she beat a retreat, smiling a sentimental smile.

At nine o'clock that night, Jenny kicked off her shoes and collapsed on her living room sofa.

The whole situation was nearly beyond comprehension. She was worried and depressed about Dad's illness, and yet inside that black cloud of worry there was this wonderful warm spot of sunshine.

Bennet loved her. He had said so—several times, in fact, in one way or another. He had gone back to the hospital with her, then taken her out for dinner.

He had called Louise to let her know what had happened. Then he had stayed close to Jenny's side, and held her hand, and kissed her good night as if he hated to leave.

Just as she hated to see him leave. When he got back from his trip, they told each other, everything might look different. Maybe. They carefully avoided talking too much about the future. But later, maybe later. . . .

Liz had called as soon as she saw Jenny's lights go on, but of course there wasn't much to report. And a message on the answering machine from Louise told her sympathetically that she was thinking of her and wishing her father well in every sense of the word. Jenny was grateful for her friends.

The day had been long, and she had a great deal to think about. But she didn't do much thinking. She was asleep as soon as her head hit the pillow.

When the sunlight crept across her bed and teased at her eyelids, she couldn't believe it was morning already. She called Dad as soon as she had drunk a cup of coffee to clear her head, and was relieved to hear the chipper note in his voice.

"I've just finished a mushy breakfast," he said. "Hospitals have a strange idea of what food is. Are you and Bennet coming by today?"

She blinked at the phone, momentarily at a loss for words. "Bennet?" she repeated, and then laughed. "Yes. He'll be coming down later before he leaves on his trip."

"You have to remember, Jenny, that while I may be ill and incapacitated, I'm not blind. I watched the two of you yesterday. You're in love, and I do like the man, you know."

"So do I, Dad."

"It showed. Incidentally, Dr. Rothke stopped by early this morning. I don't know what's going on in that man's head, but he certainly asked a lot of nosy questions. I suppose it's all necessary, and he seems like a sharp man, so I answered even the nosiest."

"Good for you. He does seem to know what he's doing. But what kind of questions did he ask?"

"He said he'd have a talk with you later. Oh, no, here comes another one of those blamed—excuse me, beautiful—nurses armed with stethoscopes and needles and bedpans. I'll see you later, then."

Jenny hung up, still smiling. Surely Dad's good mood had to be a positive sign. And she looked forward to talking to Dr. Rothke later on. Maybe he had some ideas, a new slant on things. . . .

Dr. Rothke wasn't there when Jenny got to the hospital, but Bennet was. He was hurried and apologetic, and looked torn between leaving and staying.

"I'll call as soon as I can," he told her. "Tomorrow I'll to have meetings until quite late, but I'll do my best. Oh, Jenny." He pulled her to him, burying his head in the warm, fiery fragrance of her hair. "I'm going to miss you so much."

Jenny reached up to kiss his chin, then his lips. "I'll miss you too," she whispered.

"Mushy, just like my breakfast," her father contributed in a satisfied voice. "Did you come to see me, young man, or not?"

Bennet laughed. "Of course I did. I came to see both of you. Do you approve?"

"Wholeheartedly," Dad said, and Jenny just smiled. A lot of things had been settled in that exchange, and a soft, sweet glow like warm honey took possession of her, a warmth that lasted even though Bennet had to say good-bye.

The glow only lasted until Dr. Rothke showed up later. Jenny wasn't at all prepared for the intense look on his face, the sudden formal seriousness of his manner.

Did he have bad news? That was all she could think

of that would explain his strange, distant attitude. She steeled herself for the worst when he suggested that the two of them find a quiet spot in the lounge for what he called "a discussion of Mr. Blakemore's condition."

But the last thing in the world she expected was the astonishing statement he made as soon as they were seated on the uncomfortable plastic chairs in the deserted lounge.

"There's no way to put this very pleasantly. I'm afraid I'm going to have to notify the police. It appears that someone"—he glanced up at her, then down at the floor as if disliking the statement he was making—"someone may be attempting to kill your father."

"The police? Someone trying to kill. . . ." She felt herself going pale under a chilling wave of disbelief. "What on earth are you talking about?"

He watched her closely as he dropped the bombshell that shattered the last fragile wisps of the glowing warmth she had felt earlier. "Your father is suffering from the effects of chronic arsenic poisoning."

Jenny stared at him, stupefied. Somehow, she managed to fight off the wave of hysteria that threatened to break over her with all the weight of a tidal wave. Somehow, she managed to ask intelligent questions, and to listen. She didn't like what she heard.

The next couple of days slipped by in a muddle of unreality. Between the doctor, Dad, and the police officers who came to the hospital and later to the house, she thought there must have been at least a million words exchanged.

She couldn't believe it was happening. This was the stuff of TV docudramas, something unbelievable that happened to somebody else, not to real people like Jenny or her father.

But it had happened, and it was real. The mass of words that outlined the facts began to fall into patterns, to make twisted sense. She talked to Louise briefly the next day, but she didn't try to explain the unexplainable—not at this point. She only told her that Dad was doing better.

Louise appeared to accept that, but Jenny knew that her own shock and depression showed in her voice. At that point, she wondered how they were ever going to resolve the problem. She could visualize months of investigation, the stress, the tension, the uncertainty. . . .

By the time Bennet called on the evening of the second day, those worries had been unexpectedly put to rest. She was still depressed, still felt a nagging sorrow deep in her heart. At the sound of his voice from across the country that evening, all of her hard-held control nearly exploded.

But Bennet was on the other side of the country, and she was here. She held on. At least she could tell him what had happened, and there would be time later for letting go, for crying on his shoulder if she wanted to, for being held and consoled.

"You sound a little stressed out," he observed astutely. It was his second sentence. His first had been something like hello darling, I miss you and love you. And that had helped, though her voice had shaken slightly when she answered that she felt the same—in spades.

She couldn't just pour out all that had happened, though that's what she wanted to do. *Ease into it,* she told herself, *so you can get it all out straight.*

"I'm fine, I think. How's your trip going?"

"Better than I expected. Jenny, you don't sound fine. What do you mean, you *think* you're all right? What's been going on back there?"

"You won't believe it," she told him, trying to control the catch in her voice. "I just don't know where to start."

"Is it your dad? Look, start at the beginning." His concern soothed her, even at this distance. Maybe she could tell the whole story without falling apart after all.

"Well, we know what's wrong with Dad at last, and he should get better now that we understand. It wasn't just the accident, the trauma, or a psychological thing, as we were all beginning to believe. It just aggravated those things."

"Back up a minute. What, exactly, is the mysterious 'it' you're referring to?"

"You're not going to believe this."

"Try me."

"He was being poisoned."

There was a silence at the other end of the line. Then he said, "I don't believe it."

"Neither did I. At first. And it's the first time I've ever been suspected of a crime."

"You?"

"Well, stop and think about it. Whoever was doing the cooking had to be a suspect, right? It was highly unlikely that Dad was adding poison to the food he fixed for himself. Who else did the cooking?"

"Remind me not to accept any dinner invitations from you. But that's ridiculous. Not you."

"I did, and somebody else—Liz. She often brought him tempting snacks and sandwiches and goodies—almost always when I was gone, so I wouldn't get any of it myself. She was very careful. And she was seasoning those goodies with a small dose of arsenic each time."

"Arsenic. Liz. But it doesn't make sense. Why?"

Jenny sighed. The truth had hurt, actually; she had liked Liz and trusted her. "Liz is seriously mentally ill. She had some twisted idea that she could somehow control Dad if he wasn't well, take charge, then take care of him. In her strange, irrational way, she loves him."

"How did you—how did *anybody*—ever figure all this out?"

"It fell into place when I backed off and thought about it. Dad was better during the few days before we went back to Boston for the evaluation, which Liz didn't seem to think was a great idea in the first place. She let up on the poison for a few days so no one would suspect what she was doing. And the doctors there weren't looking for arsenic. It was a foregone conclusion to them—and us—that his condition was a lingering result of the accident."

"Wait a minute. Shouldn't it have been obvious if he was being poisoned?"

"From what Dr. Rothke says, no. He hadn't seen Dad before, so he had a fresh perspective. Dad had trouble with motor control, a touchy digestion, weakness, headaches, and tingling in his hands and feet. All those symptoms are a telltale signs of chronic arsenic poisoning—plus a whitish line across the fingernails. And Dad had that. Believe me, I've learned enough about arsenic poisoning in the last few days to write a book."

"Don't tell me Liz admitted it." Bennet still sounded a little stunned and disbelieving, and she didn't blame him.

"But she did. That was the strange thing. After I talked to the police, I figured it would take months to clear it all up. Yet when they went over there, she just said yes, she'd done it, it was all for his own good, and then she went into hysterics and hasn't said much since."

"Jenny, Jenny. Oh, my poor love. Is the damage permanent?"

She really smiled then, and knew that her smile showed in her voice. "No. She darned near killed him the other night, but Dr. Rothke figured it out in time. He'll get better. He may even walk again—not like he used to, but there's a chance he'll be almost normal."

"That's the best news I've heard in a long time. For an awful lot of reasons. I just wish I was there."

"I know. Me too. But there's more."

He groaned. "I'm not sure my nervous system can stand it."

"When the police went in Liz's house, they naturally looked for arsenic in any form. You'd be surprised at how easy it is to get hold of. And guess what they found?"

"Arsenic."

"That too. But they also found Gillyflower Cottage. She had managed to spirit it across our back yards when Dad and I were in Boston. Oh, Bennet, everything's happened so quickly I feel it can't be real. Nothing seems real right now."

"*I'm* real, my sweet. And as soon as I'm back, I'll prove that to you. I wish I could be there right now."

"So do I. We'll have so much to talk about when you get back."

"We sure will. Incidentally, does my esteemed parent know about all of this yet? It'll be the most interesting thing she's heard in the past ten years, I expect."

"I talked to her this afternoon. She knows. She told me she is extremely relieved and that, if she can manage to drive her MG, she will be down to see George within the next few days." Bennet chuckled. Jenny had deliberately mimicked his mother's way of speaking, and had done it perfectly. "Apparently her back still bothers her a bit, but she said it was nothing to be concerned about."

"She'd say that regardless," he said thoughtfully. "Thank goodness Mrs. Huckaby is there." He sighed. "Well, maybe one of these days I can talk her into moving into a smaller, more convenient place. She'd be more comfortable. Hey, have I told you in the last few minutes that I love you?''

She assured him solemnly that he hadn't, and that she would like to hear all about it. The next twenty minutes were what her father would have called pleasantly ''mushy.''

Chapter Ten

Late in the afternoon, Ben slipped quietly and carefully through the small cellar window. Five pounds more and he wouldn't be able to make it.

In a way, he hated to think of leaving. There was a peace here that had soothed his troubled soul, a natural silence interspersed with bird songs and rustling breezes that had made it possible for him to breathe and think more deeply than he had in years.

Still, this wasn't his house. It had welcomed him and he had done it no harm, but it was time to leave. In his pocket was almost enough money to buy a bus ticket to another stage of his life. He hoped it was a good move.

He had seen that big dog again, padding around under the trees, probably looking for squirrels or rabbits. The dog's head and ears had gone up sharply at one point, and he had looked toward Ben as if he knew darned well where he was. Ben had hunkered down behind the remains of an old stone wall, afraid he was going to be flushed out of his hiding place like a wild animal.

But the dog only grumbled a low, unthreatening bark, as if he were trying to say hello, and ambled off. Well, he wouldn't have to worry about being spotted much longer. Though that dog, big as he was, sure wasn't the threatening type.

He had walked a long way and worked many hours for the twenty dollars in his pocket. Now that winter was right around the corner, people needed wood split. His shoulders ached and he was bone tired.

For a while, by the light of his low-wattage bulb in his cozy corner of the cellar, he pored over the newspaper he had found discarded on a garden wall, then tried a game or two of solitaire. But his eyes were bleary and wouldn't stay open. He washed up wearily and fell onto the cot he had fixed up in the corner and let the darkness and the silence soothe him into a deep sleep.

He wasn't sure, at first, what woke him up a few hours later. It was the middle of the night—but what had he heard? He rarely woke up in the night unless there was some kind of ruckus. There it was again, by gosh. It was that big dog, he was sure of it. And he had to be right outside, real close.

Ben pulled himself to his feet and slipped into his shirt and pants, peering toward the small window. The dog was right there, looking in at him, like he had done before. Only this time he was barking his head off.

One of us is in real trouble, Ben told himself. *I don't know whether it's him or me.*

He watched as the dog went down on his forepaws,

tail end still high in the air. The barking subsided suddenly when he looked the dog straight in the eye, then turned to a begging, desperate whining.

He wants something. And I don't think he's going to chew me up into little pieces.

Another series of sharp barks. "Okay, you noisy monster," Ben told him. "I'll try to trust you." He grabbed his old gray sweater and slipped slowly up through his escape window, one eye watching the dog cautiously.

But the dog just backed off a couple of steps and watched him, looking as if he was ready to run, yapping a few sharp barks that seemed to be an encouragement.

"Which one of us is crazy?" Ben asked the dog, but he didn't get an answer, because the animal had taken off down the path, looking back over his haunches at Ben as if to say, *hurry up, can't you?*

"All right, I'm coming," he yelled. He was beginning to get a strange feeling about all this. It was like one of those TV shows he used to watch years ago when his kids were little, with Lassie doing all kinds of heroic things. Only this dog would make three or four Lassies. He knew he was supposed to follow, but darned if he knew why.

Then, around a bend in the path, he could see down the gentle slope where the landscape opened out. There was a reddish glow in the sky. . . .

He broke into a desperate run, following the dog. There was a big old stone house down there. It couldn't burn, could it? It looked too big, too solid to burn, from what he had seen of it. He was wrong.

He stumbled along after the dog to the far side of the house, where a small balcony topped a square bay. Inside, through the ground-floor windows, he could see the intense flames of yellow and orange that licked at the walls, the swirls of blackness that had to be smoke.

"Is someone in there, dog?" he said softly. The dog answered by backing off a few paces and barking excitedly toward the top of the bay.

There was a woman up there. A woman wrapped in a soot-smudged gray robe. Behind her, wisps of hungry smoke tried to fight their way through a crack between the French doors that led out onto the balcony.

She came to the heavy railing of the balcony and looked down at him. "Oh, my. I am so glad to see you," she called out, her voice weak and raspy. "I seem to have a small problem here. Can you help me?"

She called this a small problem?

A heavy trellis entwined with leaves led up the side of the balcony. "Look," he shouted. "Come over the side. You can grab the trellis and let yourself down. It looks plenty strong. Hurry up!"

She looked down at him and then peered over the side of the balcony. "I am so sorry," she said with real regret, pressing her hand to her forehead before glancing back at the inferno behind her. "I seem to be very dizzy. I am not sure at all that I could manage to do that. Have you any other suggestions?"

He closed his eyes for just an instant. "I'm coming up," he called up to the woman. "I can help you over the side and then we can make it down together. I'll be right with you so you won't fall.'' He was already halfway up the trellis, and the dog was barking frantically at the base.

He had to be crazy to try this. But what else could he do? It was the only thing that would work. He reached out to help her get a foothold on the first crossbar.

Except for a few scratches from the vines and brambles, they made it to the bottom just as the sound of sirens wailed in the distance. A little late, he thought, as he led the trembling woman over to a garden bench and sank down beside her. Shock and fear had kicked in and his knees felt like they were unhinged.

''You okay?'' he asked anxiously. Her cheeks were covered with tears that wove silvery patterns through the soot as she stared at the inferno that had been her home.

''I believe I am, though just a little groggy as yet,'' she ventured, turning her head toward him. ''I cannot thank you enough. You are a knight in shining armor.''

''Well, not hardly that, now,'' he rumbled. But the words brought pride, and he squared his shoulders and sat a little straighter. He had forgotten how good praise could make a person feel.

But he had to be fair. ''The real knight has shaggy fur and a king-size bark,'' he told the soot-covered woman beside him. ''He came and got me.''

They both stared at Caesar. ''I shall buy him a very large fillet,'' Louise said. Caesar smiled.

* * *

Two weeks later, Jenny dashed home from a quick trip to pick up a couple of bottles of champagne—she knew she had forgotten something—to find that her dinner guests had already arrived.

Louise was ensconced in a comfortable easy chair, her feet on Great-Grandmother's favorite needlepoint footstool. Bennet sat on the sofa with Ben, with Dad nearby in his wheelchair. The three of them were deeply involved in a discussion of the methods of wiring miniature houses. Caesar was flopped as close as he could manage to Ben's feet, looking as if he understood every word they were saying.

Louise was listening with queenly detachment and smiled at Jenny when she burst through the door. "I do hope we didn't arrive too early?" she said half apologetically. "The promise of coq au vin and wild rice made me anxious to get here. It smells delicious, dear."

"I'm glad," Jenny answered automatically. Her eyes were on Bennet, who had risen and crossed the room to take the Champagne from her. There was an open warmth between them now and had been ever since he returned so quickly the day after the fire.

The two of them stood in the middle of the room, fingers touching lightly. There might not have been another living soul within those walls. These last several days, Jenny was wrapped in a wonderful world where Bennet's nearness sent everything else into a distant orbit. She had never known that love could be so heady, so all-consuming.

Then Ben's voice came from behind Bennet's left

shoulder and she forced herself back into the everyday, commonsense world. "I'll take those out to the kitchen, if you like," he offered.

But Jenny shook her head. "That's all right," she told him. "I have a dinner to finish up, anyway. And Bennet promised he'd make the salad."

This was, of course, an excuse for the two of them to be alone in the kitchen for a while—an excuse that was understood by everyone present, especially by the two people involved.

Bennet stood close behind Jenny as she put the finishing touches on the green bean, mushroom, and onion casserole, watching over her shoulder and then slipping his arms around her waist.

"How do you expect me to concentrate?" she grumbled.

"Concentrate on what?" He nuzzled her neck behind her ear, and she shivered. "What is it we're supposed to be doing?" He kissed her earlobe and the mushrooms skittered all over the cutting board.

She planted a quick kiss on his jawline. "Bennet, we have several people out there waiting for dinner."

"Let them order Chinese takeout. Better still, send them all out to eat someplace with very slow service."

"The salad, Bennet," she said firmly, even though his idea sounded pretty good.

"Oh, if you insist. Hey, what is that you're putting in the casserole, anyway?"

"Garlic powder. I ran out of fresh garlic—Oh, for heaven's sake. What did you think it was, arsenic?"

"Just making sure." There was a silence as he dug

the salad makings out of the refrigerator. ''Have you heard anything more about Liz?''

Jenny slid the casserole in the oven and turned to Bennet, sighing. ''It's still pretty complicated. It doesn't look as if she'll be fit to stand trial, at least not right away. For now she'll stay at Cottage Hill Hospital for treatment. When I think how close she came to killing Dad. . . .''

Tears of frustration, disappointment, and anger were still close to the surface. Bennet saw them gathering with stinging brightness at the corners of her eyes and abandoned the salad.

''It's all over now,'' he murmured, gathering her into his arms. He kissed her, then kissed her again.

It was a few minutes before she pulled away reluctantly and gestured with resignation at the countertop. ''Salad,'' she said succinctly.

''Okay, she-who-must-be-obeyed,'' he capitulated. ''But the worst really is over. Now we can think of the future, and maybe you can see Kew Gardens with me, and''—he shot her a sideways glance—''sing for me. I have great plans.''

''I'm sure you do.'' He hadn't mentioned a wedding yet as among his plans, but surely. . . . ''Finish the darned salad,'' she told him with mock asperity. ''And be sure you wash the cutting board when you're done and put the scraps down the garbage disposer.''

''Yes, *ma'am*.'' He turned away from her, grinning. She knew him pretty well. It looked as if he might have to change some of his ways. Not too many of them, but some.

* * *

Louise kept the dinner-table talk away from such disturbing topics as fire and poison. But later, after chocolate mousse and well into the second bottle of Champagne, it seemed acceptable to relax and allow the therapeutic nature of talk to take over.

Jenny was curled up very close to Bennet on the sofa, watching the flames flicker with gentle warmth in the stone fireplace. That something so welcoming and reassuring could glow within the hearth and yet cause so much trouble made her shiver.

"I'm so sorry about your house," she murmured to Louise, not for the first time, "and so glad that Ben was there."

"I probably wouldn't have made it without him," Louise said firmly over Ben's modest disclaimer. "I had taken a sleeping pill before going to bed because my back was still giving me a little trouble and I was quite groggy when I awoke. I could never have managed that trellis alone."

She fell silent for a moment, staring at the bubbles in her glass with a bemused look. "And, well, it was just a house, after all. Although I was very fond of it. I can sympathize with poor Queen Elizabeth on losing Windsor Castle." She paused thoughtfully and took a sip of her Champagne. "In a way, I am more fortunate than she, since my son is not giving me any difficulties. Right now."

Bennet growled a little, pulling Jenny even closer to him. "It's just a good thing Mrs. Huckaby was off that night,'' he said. ''If she'd been in the house, she might not have made it out.''

''I am sure Mr. Williams would have rescued her too,'' Louise proclaimed.

''Ben,'' her rescuer said. ''Please call me Ben.''

Jenny thought of the beautiful blue bedroom and sighed. ''That wonderful Belter furniture and those lamps—it's such a shame.''

''Yes.'' Louise echoed Jenny's sigh and then smiled. ''But, my dear, I do have a good memory, you know. I believe I will start on that room box we mentioned. And then, maybe, I will do one of the sitting room. I can keep the house alive that way.''

''I kept saying that wiring was aged and dangerous,'' Bennet said. ''And you wouldn't move out.''

''Well, I have now, haven't I? Although you probably weren't suggesting that I move in with you, were you? Now if you will just finish cleaning up the gatehouse, I am sure I can be quite comfortable there. Of course I expect you to move out at your earliest convenience, dear. I am sure you can find something suitable for you and. . . .'' Her voice trailed off and she seemed to think it would be a good idea to change the subject. ''Thank goodness Mr. Williams offered to stay for a week or so to help clean up and salvage what we could.''

''Ben,'' he said. ''Please.''

''Yes, of course,'' Louise agreed cheerfully. ''Thank goodness you were not a ghost after all. I am so glad you were there, Mr. Williams.''

''Ben—Well, never mind. You should be thanking

Caesar here, because if it hadn't been for him I wouldn't have known about the fire."

They all stared with rapt admiration at the dog, who by now was snoring audibly and hadn't even twitched an ear at the mention of his name.

"Have you looked at the apartment over the old garage at the gatehouse?" Louise asked Ben. "If you can fix it up it would make a lovely place to stay while I am convincing you to stay on permanently. That little room at the back of Birney House must seem a little cramped for a large man like you."

"After living in a coalhole?" Ben laughed and rubbed his hands over his face. "I don't know, Mrs. Young. I had other plans, but I'll think it over."

"She'll talk you into staying," George warned Ben. "You might as well resign yourself to that. May I please have some more Champagne, Jenny, or do I have to get up and get it myself?"

Jenny grinned at him. "I dare you," she said, getting up to refill his glass. One of these days he would probably be able to do just that. There were no promises, but the possibilities were growing stronger. They had even talked of going to the big pre-Christmas show in Springfield, and Louise had said that she would love to go along and help out.

"Do you know, I almost forgot. Louise hasn't seen the spinning wheel I've been working on for her. It's on the bench in the workroom. Jenny, why don't you go get it?"

"Yes, of course," Jenny answered, but she shot a curious look at her father. His tone of voice had been almost too casual, too rehearsed. He looked innocently back at her, and she decided she had been imagining things.

Bennet rose and followed her silently across the living room, and Jenny stopped in the doorway to look back. There were strange, secretive smiles on every face, including Bennet's. What was up, anyway? What did they know that she didn't?

"What's going on?" she whispered to Bennet, but he just gave her a gentle push, his face carefully blank.

"Go get the spinning wheel, Jenny," he told her. Well, that was the logical thing to do. She would find out sooner or later.

She stopped suddenly with her hand at the light switch. The workroom was dark, except for one room box, her favorite, the Regency bedroom. She could have sworn she hadn't left the tiny lights on in it. Just yesterday she had added a formal arrangement of flowers to the side table.

Without turning on the overhead light, she gravitated as if hypnotized to the shelf where the miniature bedroom glowed with an inviting air. The candles in the sconces were lit, and a minute orange light nestled among the logs in the classical fireplace flickered just as it should. But what on earth had happened?

A dressing gown that had been placed precisely over the back of a chair lay in a heap across the chest at the foot of the bed. Half-inch silver hairbrushes, once lined up with military precision, were scattered among overturned bottles on the dressing table; wine bottles and glasses on a silver tray were also upended. That looked like a pile of dirty laundry in the corner. And what on earth was that huge piece of paper jutting out from under the edge of the floral-patterned rug?

"My, my," Bennet's voice came from behind her. "What have we here? We shall have to call the valet to clear this up. It appears the inhabitant of the room has made a huge mess."

He was behind this. He had to be.

"Slob," she said grimly. "Why?"

"I think you should investigate the paper on the floor," Bennet suggested.

Jenny unlatched the hinged frame front and eased it open, reaching for the paper. Once she had slipped it carefully out of the room, the huge piece of paper wasn't so big. In fact, it was quite small, folded over, written on in tiny letters. It had just looked enormous in that perfect one-inch-scale room.

She unfolded the paper, darting a dirty look at Bennet as she did so. Holding it close to the gentle light from the room box, she read it aloud: "*Just stopped by, as you can see, to ask if you will marry me.*"

She stood in dazed silence for a moment, not knowing whether to laugh or to cry.

"I'm sorry," Bennet said.

"Sorry?" she asked on a hiccup.

"I tried to get it in scale with the room, but I can't write that small. And I had to do all this while you went out to get the Champagne, so I didn't make as much of a mess as I'd intended. I hope you don't mind. I'll try to do better next time."

"Bennet Young, you're crazy."

"This is true. Well, will you?"

"Will I what?"

"Marry me, silly."

"Of course I will. If you promise to learn to pick up your socks."

There were several long, silent moments in the darkness of the room while they clung together, sealing promises in a traditional way. Jenny could have sworn at one point that she heard a vague stirring and whispering over toward the door, but the sound melted away.

That was all right, Jenny thought as she caught her breath. If they had had an audience for a few moments, it was fine. That particular audience had helped to engineer this whole thing, after all. She hoped they had enjoyed the final scene.

Though it wasn't the final scene, she reminded herself. It was just the beginning.